W9-CRM-435

Stolen Past

Tara Randel

Annie's®
AnniesFiction.com

Library of Congress-in-Publication Data
Stolen Past/ by Tara Randel
p. cm.
I. Title
                    2016961007

AnniesFiction.com
(800) 282-6643
Amish Inn Mysteries™
Series Creator: Shari Lohner
Series Editor: Jane Haertel
Cover Illustrator: Kelley McMorris

10 11 12 13 14 | Printed in China | 9 8 7 6 5 4 3 2 1

1

Liz Eckardt, owner of the Olde Mansion Inn, cautiously made her way down the wide staircase, juggling a big box of Independence Day decorations.

"Can I help you?" her employee, Sarah Borkholder, rushed to ask as Liz plopped down the box on the shiny wood floor once she reached the foyer. Sarah, always ready and willing to pitch in with Liz's projects, was dressed in her usual gray dress with a white apron and black *Kapp*.

"There's only one more." Liz puffed out a breath. "I can handle it."

A faraway look sparkled in Sarah's eyes. "I remember when the previous owners decorated the inn for the Fourth of July. Every year we would drive by in our buggy and look at the beautiful red, white, and blue displays. The inn was so sad without any decorations when they left. It will be wonderful to see the banners flying outside again."

Liz absently brushed a strand of hair from her eye. "We only have three weeks until the big blowout. We've had so many guests, this is the first free moment I've had to scour the storage room."

"Speaking of scouring, I should get to my chores."

Since Liz had bought the inn, a three-story Victorian bed-and-breakfast with six guest rooms, she'd been busier than she'd ever imagined. After leaving the structured world of corporate law, she now loved the freedom of meeting new people, running her own business, and coming up with new breakfast ideas. Settling in Pleasant Creek, Indiana, had been quite a lifestyle change from Boston, but the townsfolk had embraced her, not only because of her newfound familial connections to the local Amish community, but because this place was special. It was small-town America at its best. Liz couldn't wait to celebrate the Fourth of July this year.

"In a minute. Let's go through the box first." Flipping open the flap, Liz peered inside. "Looks like the banners you were talking about. Let's pull them out."

With Sarah's assistance, Liz unfolded four red, white, and blue half-moon buntings with metal eyelets.

"We'll hang these on the front porch." Liz rummaged through the box and found a dozen small flags, which would do nicely to line the sidewalk. "And add these out front on the big day." She dug deeper and found twisted ribbons with metallic stars attached. She held one up. "What are these?"

"Dizzy danglers," Sarah informed her. "See how it spins around when you hold it?"

Liz laughed. "I'll hang these by the front door." She scanned the now empty box. "That's it."

"Don't forget the store window shades," Mary Ann Berne said as she exited Sew Welcome, the fabric- and quilting-supply store that was housed on the main level of the inn. The windows faced Main Street, which would showcase the patriotic-themed shades Mary Ann and her business partner, Sadie Schwarzentruber, had designed and manufactured. "Sadie and I will do our share."

"Then we should be set." Liz placed her hands on her hips. "I still have one more box to retrieve, but am I missing anything?"

"Sugar cookies with red and blue sprinkles," Sadie said as she joined them. Always a sharp if eccentric dresser, today she sported a plum-colored fedora with a colorful pheasant feather attached.

"Already on the list," Liz told her.

"And don't forget, the inn is part of the Heritage Day tour," Sadie said.

"Jackson mentioned it to me, but I haven't had time to sit down and get the details." Pleasant Creek's mayor, Jackson Cross, had talked to her a few days earlier when they bumped into each other at the coffee shop, but that was as far as the conversation had gotten.

"Some of the residents with historic or high-profile homes within walking distance of downtown open their doors once a year. The proceeds go to charity. All you need to do is share a little history about the inn and give folks a brief tour of the ground floor," Mary Ann said.

"And cookies. Don't forget the cookies."

Liz chuckled. Seventy-something Sadie wasn't in the least bit forgetful. In fact, she was usually the first to remind Liz of something she'd forgotten.

Brushing her neatly cut, silver-gray hair behind one ear, Mary Ann said, "It's good for business. For all of us."

Liz nodded. "I've got the complete history of the inn recorded on the computer in my office. I can print out copies and come up with a giveaway for tourists who stop by." She pushed back the sleeves of her blouse. "Time for the next box."

She climbed the stairs to the second floor. Passing the open door of the Somewhere in Time Room, she heard Sarah humming as she went about her chores. A smile crossed her lips. Liz hadn't thought she'd be so happy owning an inn, but here she was, humming along with Sarah as she stepped inside the storage room. She grabbed the other box and returned downstairs. Mary Ann and Sadie still waited in the foyer.

"No customers today, ladies?" Liz asked.

"Not yet, but Miriam's class starts soon." Mary Ann glanced at her watch. "She should be here by now."

A tendril of worry coiled through Liz. Ever since finding out Miriam Borkholder was her late mother's cousin, Liz had become part of a large, extended Amish family. It was a dream come true for an only child. While Liz didn't adhere to the *Ordnung*, that is, the Amish order, she'd grown close to Miriam and her children, often driving out to their home or visiting whenever Miriam came to Sew Welcome to teach a class using her treadle sewing machine. Miriam, always so conscientious about her classes, rarely came late. And if she did, her family was usually the reason. Could something serious be keeping Miriam this time?

"We've been busy shelving new merchandise from today's delivery," Sadie informed her. "Since we installed the newfangled inventory system on the computer, I'm still learning how to use it."

Mary Ann laughed. "She picked it up faster than I did."

"Makes things easier, I must say. One needs to keep up with technology," Sadie said sagely.

Liz agreed. She had programs on her computer to organize reservations, help her with Internet marketing, and track kitchen inventory.

"How did we ever get along before computers?" Mary Ann asked, her tone dry.

The front door opened and two chatting women made their way to the shop.

"Students," Sadie announced, then followed them into the shop.

"And three more signed up yesterday," Mary Ann chimed in.

Sew Welcome didn't need much marketing. The store and its owners had a far-reaching reputation and fan base, bringing in repeat customers to the store and, as a result, to the inn.

"Miriam will be here," Liz assured her friends, hoping she was right. "When has she ever let you down?"

Before Mary Ann could reply, the front door opened and Miriam hurried inside. Her cheeks were red and her black *Kapp* was slightly askew until she set it back in place.

"We were getting worried," Mary Ann said, her eyes wide. Miriam was never harried.

"I am terribly sorry. Philip had . . . Well, we left the *Haus* late."

Liz picked up on the slight pause. "Is everything okay?" She knew Miriam would most likely keep any troubles to herself. She'd made it clear to Liz that the Amish did not share their concerns with the English, the Amish name for people outside their community, but that didn't keep Liz from asking.

"It will be fine." She smoothed her apron. "I should get inside."

As she rushed into the store, Liz exchanged a glance with Mary Ann. "Far from fine, if those worry lines on her forehead are any indication."

Mary Ann shrugged. "If anyone can get her to talk, it's you."

"I'll try to catch her after class, but right now, I have another box to unpack."

"Have fun," Mary Ann called over her shoulder as she returned to the store.

Liz opened the flaps to find smaller doodads inside. There were a couple of figurines of men in old-time uniforms, one playing a fife, the other playing a drum. She carefully placed them back inside and carried the box to the sitting room. Considering the room for a moment, she decided to place the figurines on the fireplace mantel, pausing a moment to run a finger over the framed photo of her mother. Sadness swamped her as it did whenever she viewed the photo. She still missed her mother, and thought of her every day. She silently thanked her mother for the gift she'd left behind after her death: the diary that had been instrumental in bringing Liz to Pleasant Creek.

Shaking off her somberness, she continued her search through the box. There were more figurines, a sparkly centerpiece resembling a burst of fireworks, and a beautiful wreath festooned with holiday ribbon for the front door.

After placing the final article in its designated spot, she stepped back to view her handiwork.

"Not bad, if I do say so myself."

"Talking to yourself again?"

Liz spun around to find Naomi Mason, owner of Sweet Everything, the bakery located next door to the inn. Her dark curly hair was pulled back, and she wore an amused grin.

"Let me guess," said Liz. "You're off for the day and decided to come over here and heckle me."

Naomi pointed to her signature coral-colored apron. "Just a short break. I realized I needed thread for the patriotic streamers I'm making for the bakery."

"Streamers?"

"Yes. I thought about crepe paper, but I don't like the look. Since I make my baked goods from scratch, I'm afraid that goes for my decorations too."

"I like the idea, but this year I just haven't had the time. I found buntings just this afternoon."

"Opal must have caught my sewing bug. She mentioned that she had made a patriotic banner for George so he can hang it at the train display on Heritage Day."

Opal and George Ringenberg were longtime residents of Pleasant Creek.

"The more I hear about Heritage Day, the more I think I should be involved."

"There's a ton to do. Check by town hall. I believe they have someone stationed there heading the volunteer committee."

"Goodness, everyone takes this seriously."

"It's a big day for the town businesses, both financially and for publicity reasons. The event keeps growing bigger every year, bringing new faces to Pleasant Creek from all over the region."

That explained why Jackson Cross wanted the inn to be part of the tour, even if he hadn't given her specific details yet. He was as busy as everyone else in town; more so since he was the mayor. As she heard more, she resolved to do her fair share. "I guess we all have the upcoming holiday on our minds."

"Yes." Naomi's gaze flitted to the clock in the foyer. "Gotta run." Naomi waved and rushed into the fabric store.

Liz glanced at her own watch. Just an hour until the afternoon check-in. She gathered up the paper wrappings and collected the boxes to return to storage, then joined Sarah in the kitchen. Beans, an English bulldog and permanent inn resident, opened his eyes a slit when her entrance interrupted his perpetual nap.

"The tea is ready," the young woman informed her.

Liz washed up at the sink. "Did you start the cookies?"

Sarah nodded to the bowl on the counter. "Just mixed up the ingredients."

"Once they start baking, it won't take long before Sadie finds an excuse to make her way here."

"She'll be looking for a tea bag."

"Or to heat up water."

They both laughed. Sadie might be a live wire, but some of her habits were rather predictable. Since Sarah had everything under control, Liz headed back to her quarters to change out of her work clothes. Before she made it there, she ran into Naomi again in the foyer.

"Got what you needed?"

"Hmm." She glanced at Liz and blinked. "Oh yes."

"What is it with everyone today? First Miriam came in distracted and now you."

"It's nothing."

Liz waited. While Naomi was all smiles a few minutes earlier, now a frown wrinkled her forehead. Clearly "it" was something.

"You're going to think I'm crazy."

"After all we've been through?"

The two women, along with Mary Ann, Sadie, and their other friends, Caitlyn Ross and Opal, were part of a quilting group called the Material Girls. They came together to quilt, plan special projects, or just to spend time together. They had also solved a few mysteries in Pleasant Creek since Liz moved to town, strengthening their special bond.

"True." Naomi bit her bottom lip, then spoke, "I'm missing a sign at the bakery."

"What do you mean, 'missing'?"

"You know the grouping of pictures on the back wall?"

Liz knew the spot. She'd noticed the collection the first time she'd stopped at the bakery. It had started with just a few kitschy wall hangings about coffee or bakery treats, and some plaques with pithy sayings, but soon Naomi began collecting vintage prints and signs that took over the corner and, with time, spread out along the bakery walls.

"So which one is missing?"

"The original Pleasant Creek Bakery sign. Remember, I found it when we went to the Wilfreds' estate sale?"

Liz nodded. It was a square piece of porcelain with lettering aged over the years, leaving it with a faded patina. It read: "Pleasant Creek Bakery, established 1890. A pleasant place to buy bread and sweets."

"You were so excited to bring the original back to the bakery," Liz said.

"It's my favorite piece." Naomi's brow furrowed. "I move the hangings around from time to time if I've acquired something new and need the space. This morning, when I was cleaning a table after some breakfast customers, I looked up and noticed it was gone."

"Naomi, who would take a sign off your wall and then walk out the door with it?"

"My thoughts exactly."

"So maybe you misplaced it?"

"I rearranged a grouping last week, moving the sign from its original position, but I didn't notice anything amiss until this morning."

"Could one of your employees have moved it?"

"Candice is in today and she hasn't noticed anything out of the ordinary. I won't see Jenny until tomorrow."

"There has to be a logical answer." Liz thought for a moment. "Is it in the back room?"

"Checked. Nowhere to be found." Naomi frowned. "I'll be bummed if someone stole it."

"If someone did, when would they have had the opportunity to swipe it without you noticing?"

"Tourist season is in full swing, so I've been busy. Plus, the seniors come over from the center and hang out a couple mornings a week, not that I suspect them. It could have happened anytime."

"Or it's simply been misplaced."

"I hope. I won't ever find an original like that again."

Liz patted her friend on the shoulder. "It'll turn up."

"In the meantime I should get back to work. I have two special orders I need to get started on before I close for the night."

After her friend left, Liz went to her room to change her clothes. How on earth could Naomi's sign have gone missing? Naomi was right. The summer tourist population had picked up in Pleasant Creek. The inn bookings were steady through August, so Liz understood being busy. But could the bakery be too hectic for the owner to notice a vintage sign had gone missing?

For her friend's sake, Liz hoped it was some sort of mix-up.

She donned a bright short-sleeved blouse and denim skirt, and headed into the library of the inn, which also served as her office. There were plenty of keepsakes that Liz would miss if they disappeared from the inn. She'd come into possession of some beautiful pieces when she bought the place and had picked up more since arriving in town. Each themed guest room had special touches she'd personally placed there. Would she notice if a trinket or two went missing?

Suddenly a mental inventory popped up in her mind's eye. Liz had cleaned the rooms with Sarah this morning and didn't recall anything out of place, but she made a note to inspect each room again when she had a minute.

Liz had just turned on the computer when the door opened and voices carried in from the foyer. *My guests*, Liz thought. She was expecting two retired sisters from Pennsylvania who were going to share the Rose of Sharon Room. Soon, a middle-aged couple from Chicago would be checking in as well. Liz planned to place them in the Heirloom Room. She stood, preparing to welcome the sisters. Thoughts of missing objects would have to wait.

2

"Liz, what is your favorite shop in town?"

Pouring a cup of coffee the next morning for Joanne, one of the visiting sisters, Liz considered the question. "I guess it depends on what I'm looking for. What are you interested in?"

"Old books," Dotty, the other sister, replied.

"Oh yes," Joanne said. "And how about vintage clothing?"

"Once Upon a Tale for books. Retreads for vintage apparel," Liz replied. "And there's also Soap and Such. They carry a wonderful selection of bath products. I love that shop."

"We'll definitely check it out. Our entire day is dedicated to shopping." Joanne giggled. "Our husbands don't like when we travel together."

Liz moved to the next table. "And how about you, Mr. and Mrs. Stanton?"

"Please, call me Tori," Mrs. Stanton said. "Window shopping for me. Dave is interested in the architecture around town. He's an amateur photographer."

"Interesting. What are your favorite types of subjects?" Liz asked Dave.

"Old buildings. Landscapes."

"Not people?"

"Not unless they happen to be in range when I'm making a photograph. But as a favorite, no."

"I think you'll find plenty to catch your eye here in Pleasant Creek."

"That's the reason we came here." Tori cradled a coffee cup in her hands. "I stumbled upon an Internet article about your town, then checked out several guidebooks. This charming place is exactly what Dave was hoping to find."

"It's true," her husband agreed. "Then I read about the clock tower with the four clock faces in the square and I was hooked. I'm intrigued by the buildings with the Swiss-style balconies and also the tall church steeple. Fascinating."

"Don't forget the flower boxes in the business windows," Tori added. "I noticed every color imaginable blooming as we drove down Main Street."

"Pleasant Creek is a pretty town," Liz agreed.

"And when we drove in," Tori went on, "we passed acres and acres of farmland before crossing over a covered bridge. I'm afraid two days won't be enough time for Dave to snap pictures of everything."

"You're always welcome to stay longer," Liz pitched. "We have a lot to be proud of here. You'll also have to check out the rich history of the surrounding area while you're here."

"We'll certainly try." Tori finished her coffee before rising. "Ready, Dave?"

"Let me run upstairs for my camera."

"Enjoy your day," Liz called after them.

Soon after the Stantons left, the sisters announced that they, too, were ready to explore the town. "Oh, and Liz," Dotty said, "we love the Rose of Sharon Room. The quilts are beautiful, and the vintage furniture is right up our alley."

"I'm so pleased you like it. The quilts are handmade, you know."

"I could tell, having sewn a few quilts myself."

Joanne rummaged around in her purse. "Just making sure I have my credit cards before we go."

Dotty rolled her eyes. "They're in her wallet. She'll check fifty times before we leave."

"I heard you. And I won't check that often. Maybe ten times."

Dotty sent Liz an "I told you so" look.

"You ladies enjoy yourselves. The weather is still pleasant enough that you can be outside the entire day without wilting in the heat."

"We will. And thanks for the recommendations."

Once the dining room cleared out, Liz started cleaning up.

"Your Tuscan egg dish was a success," Sarah told her as she gathered up the food platters.

"I wasn't sure about it, but the guests ate it up. I'll serve it again this weekend."

"Speaking of this weekend, will you be needing me?"

Sarah occasionally worked on a Saturday if the inn was busy. Liz tried not to call her in too often since Sarah spent the weekends catching up on chores at her own home.

"I think I can manage. Plans?"

"No. It is a family matter."

Liz shot her a glance. Sarah was married to Miriam's son. And since Miriam had been vague about the reason for her tardiness yesterday, Liz wondered again what might be going on at the Borkholder residence.

"Anything I can do to help?"

"We will handle it."

So much for getting any information. Miriam and her family were always so closemouthed. How could Liz help them, as she had in the past, if she didn't know their circumstances? Perhaps when things calmed down Sarah or Miriam would fill her in.

Later that morning, Liz carried a handful of fresh towels from the laundry to the currently unoccupied Amish Room to get ready for the next incoming guests. With the sisters and the Stantons out touring the town, she had some much-needed time to catch up on menus, supply lists, and reservation requests while the morning was quiet. Being an inn owner meant she had never-ending responsibilities. But Liz was more than up for the job.

After depositing the towels in the bathroom, she roamed the Amish Room. She especially loved the patchwork quilt with the appliquéd silhouettes of Amish figures. This was probably her most requested room, and why not? The theme fit right in with the charm of Pleasant Creek's Amish community. With a contented sigh, she closed the door behind her and hurried back downstairs. No more procrastinating. Paperwork would not get itself done. But first, she had a prearranged appointment to talk to her godson, Steve, via video chat.

As she waited for the computer to boot up, she opened a window to let in some fresh air. It was a beautiful June day, but July was just around the corner and was sure to bring with it the usual humidity and high temperatures. Liz drank in the sweet scent of the roses planted outside. Not far away, she could see a hummingbird thrumming among the deep pink blooms of columbine. A steady breeze carried in the clean, fresh air. She inhaled, not missing the big city one little bit.

Returning to the keyboard, she pulled up the video-chat application and waited.

"Hey, Mom," Steve's rich voice filled the room.

Even though Steve wasn't biologically her son, she'd raised him from the time his parents died in an auto accident when he was seven, and she loved him as if he were her own.

"Steve." She upped the volume. "How are you?"

"Busy. Lucky to have a few minutes of downtime."

"Anything exciting going on?"

"Nothing you'd be interested in, but I do have news."

"Good or bad?"

"Looks like I'm up for a short deployment."

Her stomach dropped. As proud as she was that Steve had chosen to serve his country, it took her breath away every time he had to go to another foreign location. "Oh, Steve. I'd hoped you could come to Pleasant Creek. We're getting ready for a big Fourth of July celebration."

"Normally I would have gotten leave, but I'm needed on this particular operation."

"And I suppose I won't be able to reach you?"

"Not sure right now, but you know I'll call when I can."

She kept her sigh quiet. He didn't need to hear her disappointment. "You know I'll be praying for you and your unit."

"Thanks. And I promise we'll get together soon."

"I'm going to hold you to that."

They chatted a few more minutes before Steve had to go. As Liz signed off, she silently prayed for her son's safety. She knew it was selfish, but a part of her hoped he'd choose to re-enter civilian life soon.

The next hour flew by as she took care of business matters. Covering a yawn, she sat back in the chair and stretched the kink that had formed in her back. A gust of wind suddenly rustled her papers, tossing a few sheets to the floor. Her penholder toppled, pens and pencils cascading over her desk.

"Good grief." She caught the writing implements before they rolled over the side, then reached down for the papers. Retrieving the rest of her materials, she placed them back on the desk, just as another gust whipped through the room. Curious, she glanced out the window. Tree limbs swung a bit more heartily than when she'd first started working. Was a storm ready to blow through town?

Liz reached over to the nearby bookshelf for a paperweight, an antique silver and cobalt-blue glass inkwell the Material Girls had given to her as a gift when she opened the inn. Her hand closed on empty air. She glanced over to see if she'd missed her target, but the inkwell she normally kept there was gone. Liz rose from the chair and searched the top of the bookshelf. No inkwell. Crouching down, she searched the remaining shelves. Nothing. She checked her desk drawers. Still nothing.

Moving to close the window halfway against the blowing wind, she recalled Naomi's visit yesterday. The missing sign. At the time, Liz had wondered how Naomi could misplace it, but now that her paperweight was gone, she understood her friend's situation.

"Maybe Sarah moved it," she said to the empty room. Not that Sarah would ever do so without a reason, but Liz had to check.

But she couldn't find Sarah either. "Please tell me I didn't misplace my employee too."

"Did you say something, Miss Eckardt?" Sarah asked as she walked into the kitchen from the utility room.

"Just wondering where you were."

"Emptying the trash. Did you need something?"

"I have a quick question. Have you tidied up around my work desk lately?"

"No. I know you have a certain way you keep your forms and books and things, so I stay clear."

"Hmm."

"You have that look on your face."

Liz started. "What look?"

"The one you get when you are worried about something."

Liz waved her hand. "It's nothing."

"You are sure?"

"Yes. And speaking about being worried, I've been wanting to ask how your family is doing, but I didn't want to pry. Is everything okay at home?"

"We will be fine. You know family sticks together."

Liz did. Until the Borkholders decided to share, Liz would have to accept her place outside of the loop. "You know I'm here if you need anything."

Sarah nodded, but kept busy with her chores instead of continuing the conversation. Liz decided she might as well get on with her search for the missing inkwell.

Determined to tear her work area apart if necessary, she crossed the rotunda on her way back to the library. Mary Ann strode out of Sew Welcome, muttering something. When she noticed Liz, she stumbled to a halt.

"I almost ran you over," Liz told her friend.

"Sorry. I was lost in thought."

"Seems to be going around."

Mary Ann raised a questioning brow.

Liz decided not to elaborate. "What's up?"

"I lost some merchandise in the store."

Mary Ann losing inventory? Hardly. The woman knew every inch of the store like the back of her hand. "You and Sadie know every piece of your inventory."

"We do, but this was a special order. I logged it into the computer, but I'm not sure where Sadie stored it."

It wasn't like Sadie to stow an order somewhere her business partner couldn't find it. Something was definitely wrong. "So is it lost or misplaced?"

"Is there a difference?" Mary Ann frowned. "It's an antique thimble collection. I had a customer mention her interest. Althea Mitchell happened to have one, so I bought it to resell. It originally belonged to the wife of an early mayor of Pleasant Creek."

Of course Althea had a collection of thimbles. Her house was like a museum.

Mary Ann continued. "Her husband dropped off the box last week, and the customer is coming in today to pick it up. What will I tell her?"

"Maybe you should check with Sadie before you panic."

"True. It's just that I've never had this happen before."

"Join the club." She went on to explain about Naomi's vanishing vintage sign and her missing paperweight. After she finished, Liz couldn't ignore the prickly sensation traversing her skin. "I don't normally believe in coincidences. Do you think I have a thief at the inn?"

"I'd hate to think so," Mary Ann said.

Liz worried her lower lip. "Let's each take one more look, then we can decide if we need to take it to the police."

Liz raced back to her desk and searched the entire area once more. She even moved the desk and pulled the shelf from its place against the wall to see if the inkwell had fallen behind. All she found were a few dust bunnies.

Discouraged, she met Mary Ann back in the store. "No luck."

"Me neither. I called Sadie but she's not answering her phone." Mary Ann moved behind the checkout counter and picked up the phone to try again. "Still no answer."

"Where is Sadie anyway? She's always here at opening time."

"That's another thing that has me worried. I called both her landline and cell phone numbers." Mary Ann's brow angled. "Maybe I should run by her house. I do worry about her living alone in that big house at her age."

"She's so lively, I think we take her health for granted."

Just then the shop door flew open. Sadie coasted inside, her eyes alight with excitement.

"Sadie. Where were you? We were worried," Liz scolded.

Sadie brushed off her concern. "Big news."

"I've been trying to reach you on the phone," Mary Ann said. "We have a problem and I need to talk to you."

"Can it wait a minute?" Sadie looked about ready to burst.

"Tell us already," Liz urged, recognizing the look.

"The wagon wheel outside the courthouse has gone missing," Sadie said in a rush.

"What?" Mary Ann's mouth dropped. "When?"

"Nobody is sure. Some folks say they saw it yesterday or the day before, others swear it went missing days ago."

Liz and Mary Ann exchanged incredulous glances.

"It's the buzz all over town. I think Bert Worth is about to have a heart attack."

Bert, retired town clerk and self-appointed town historian, was setting up a display in the courthouse lobby featuring town history and memorabilia for the Heritage Day celebration.

Mary Ann turned to Liz. "That wheel is the cornerstone of Pleasant Creek's history. When three of the founding fathers went to the state capitol building to get the town charter, they almost didn't make it back. The wheel broke, and they fought off an ambush."

"Which is why its disappearance is the talk of the town," Sadie said.

"That wagon wheel is big," Liz said. "How could someone take it without anyone noticing?"

"Not sure, but Jackson didn't look very happy. He was standing outside the building with Bert and a crowd was gathering. A reporter had just pulled up when I drove away."

Liz knew for sure Jackson would not like the suggestion of a scandal. He took his position as mayor very seriously but was notoriously closemouthed with the press.

"How did you find out?" Liz asked.

"Please. Nothing gets past me. I have an information network the president of the United States would be jealous of."

Liz chuckled. Sadie spoke the truth.

"I guess it's time to call the chief," Mary Ann told Liz.

Sadie perked up. "Chief Houghton? Why?"

"I can't find the thimble collection. We're supposed to sell it to the buyer today."

"But I put the box behind the counter for safekeeping," Sadie assured her.

"That's the first place I looked. It's gone."

"I'm missing the antique inkwell you ladies gave me," Liz said thoughtfully. "When you surprised me with it, didn't you say it was used as part of the celebration held when Pleasant Creek's founding fathers returned with the original town charter, and the document was signed by the new town officials?"

"That's right," Sadie said. "When I discovered the inkwell was being sold, I knew you'd love having a piece of Pleasant Creek history. I bought it right out from under Bert Worth's nose."

"Naomi's missing a vintage sign at the bakery," Liz said.

"Good grief." Sadie's eyes widened. "What on earth is going on in Pleasant Creek?"

"Seems someone is helping themselves to our history," Liz said, surprised by her own words.

3

"It's more than just our three businesses," Sadie informed the Material Girls as they sat together in Sew Welcome on Wednesday night, brainstorming ideas for their next quilting project. There were no classes scheduled, so the women had the shop to themselves. They'd gathered chairs near the fabric section to visit, discuss town events, and to get the details of the thefts. As usual, Sadie had the lowdown.

"Many of the Main Street businesses have had thefts: a box of old type from the print shop, a handheld date stamper from the library, and an antique bottle from Bontrager's Family Drugstore. Although not old, a book about town history was taken from the bookstore." Sadie shook her head. "Someone even lifted an old gavel that had belonged to a former judge right out of the mayor's office. Cheeky, if you ask me."

"Apparently, whoever is taking the items isn't too concerned about the legalities," twenty-something Caitlyn Ross added drily.

"It doesn't make sense," Opal said. "Burglaries are rare in Pleasant Creek. There may have been some teenagers shoplifting, but nothing on this level."

"And so specific," Mary Ann said. "So far it sounds like everything that has been taken is old or somehow related to town history."

"I'll bet the phone has been ringing off the hook at the police station." Liz closed the craft magazine she was leafing through and placed it on her lap. "The chief was pretty busy when I got hold of him."

"I know what you mean," Naomi said. "He didn't even take a free pastry when he came to the bakery to get my statement. Not at all like the man."

"I hope this is settled by Heritage Day. We don't need this hanging over the town on one of our biggest tourist days," Sadie grumbled.

"The chief is investigating as we speak, so let's get back on the topic of our project." Mary Ann always had a way of reining in the women. She was a natural leader and calming presence whenever the women were stirred up over a new mystery or project idea. "We don't have anything new planned."

Naomi rolled her shoulders. "I'm sorry, girls, but with the big celebration coming up, I'm swamped. I'm sponsoring a booth, so I have lots of sweets to bake between now and then."

"I'm helping George's train club this year," Opal said. "He's been after me for years to be involved. Honestly, the man doesn't ask much, and he's always supportive of our projects. I want to be there for him."

"We're manning the information booth," Sadie reminded Mary Ann.

"The hospital will have a presence too," Caitlyn said. "The nursing staff volunteered a shift. We're handing out bottled water."

"And I have to open the inn for a town tour." Liz pushed down the alarm that had clung to her since news of the thefts had reached her. "The inn is booked solid."

"Sounds like we're all too busy for a project right now." Mary Ann tapped a finger against her lips. "How about something for back-to-school time? It's still a few months away, and after the excitement of Heritage Day dies down, we'd still have time to get something together."

Caitlyn perked up. "A back-to-school giveaway? Maybe we could sew quilted pencil cases and donate them to the Community Church. They always help with some kind of local school project."

Sadie clasped her hands together. "Sounds wonderful. If we start soon, we can get plenty of cases made in time for the next school season."

"So, are we in agreement?" Mary Ann asked.

The women nodded eagerly.

"Very well," said Mary Ann. "I'll pick out material with fun patterns, and we can set up cutting and sewing duties after we fulfill our Heritage Day obligations."

"Now that the meeting is over," Sadie said, "let's get back to dishing about the town."

"The more I think about it, the more I have to wonder what the thief is thinking." Opal's brow furrowed. "Why antiques and why now?"

Naomi stood and began to tidy up what was left of the snacks, her footsteps echoing on the hardwood floor as she moved along the counter. "This stealing spree must have been well thought out for the thief to collect so many goods in such a short period of time. No one can remember anything odd or seeing a stranger poking around before we discovered so many stores had been hit."

As the ladies stood to help and gathered their purses, Liz and Mary Ann pushed the chairs back to the long table against the wall, where a row of sewing machines sat. "And the thief knew which businesses had something of interest to steal. Or at least what was important to the folks he or she stole from."

Sadie went behind the counter to close out the cash register. "Like Mary Ann said, this is very specific."

"Who in Pleasant Creek would understand the significance of these items?" Liz asked the group.

"Bert," came Sadie's quick reply. "But he loves the history of this town. He'd never steal a thing, not when he could ask and most everyone would gladly donate their antiques."

"How is his display coming?" Liz queried. "I talked to him when he first started the project but haven't bumped into him since."

"George talked to him last week," Opal said. "He'll be spending the next week setting up the exhibit before the big day. He also got the okay from the town council to extend the exhibit indefinitely."

Sadie chuckled. "Bert has been waiting his entire life for this opportunity. I can't think of anyone more loyal to Pleasant Creek than that gentleman."

With a frown, Opal said, "For his sake, and everyone else's, let's hope the chief finds a lead on the culprit soon, or there might not be enough of Pleasant Creek's history left for an exhibit."

———————*///////////////////////////////*———————

Friday morning, any business owner who'd had an item disappear sat around a long table or stood along the wall in the conference room at the courthouse.

Liz was stunned by the turnout. How had the thief managed to collect such a big haul without getting caught?

Philip Borkholder was standing in the back, dressed in a light shirt and dark pants, his straw hat in his hands. Taciturn as always, he was close-lipped about why he was there, but Liz was able to get a little information out of him. Some of his *Werkzeugs*, tools, had been taken right out of his wagon when he'd parked outside Cross Furniture. *Perhaps that explains Miriam's frazzled state the other day.*

Even Rob Carver, reporter for the *Pleasant Creek News & Views*, made it to the meeting, but Liz figured he was there for a story. This certainly qualified as front-page news.

Jackson entered the room. Liz couldn't ignore how good he looked in a navy-blue button-down shirt and khakis, despite his weary expression. Just as quickly as she'd begun to admire his appearance, she stopped herself. Like everyone else, she was here to discuss a serious problem, not linger over the mayor's wardrobe choice. Or his handsome face. Or anything else about the man. *Sheesh.*

"Thank you for coming," Jackson said, his tone and gaze serious. "I've received a list of stolen items from Chief Houghton, and we're doing everything we can to locate your belongings. I appreciate your patience in the matter."

"Any leads?" Rob asked right off the bat.

"As of today, no. The only thing you have in common is that you were victims and that the items had more personal meaning than resale value."

"Everything seems to be tied to town history," Sadie announced from her seat next to Liz.

"Yes, you're right," Jackson said.

"How will this affect Heritage Day?" Rob asked, probably fishing for a quote he could use in the newspaper. "This is important for the town."

"I agree. The best thing we can do right now is let the chief do his job. His officers also have the list and will contact you when they discover your items," Jackson said.

"Suppose they don't?" Rob asked in his stirring-up-trouble tone.

Liz noticed Jackson barely hide a grimace. He was in a tough position right now, with people demanding answers he couldn't provide.

"With the number of belongings taken, I can't imagine they will stay hidden long. Trying to sell any of them would be a big giveaway to the culprit's identity. Especially the wagon wheel, which is big. Any attempts to fence something like that won't go unnoticed."

"But the thief could hide it well enough in a barn," Sadie said. "Or warehouse, or automotive garage, or—"

"Sadie," Jackson warned.

She crossed her arms over her chest. "I'm just saying."

Liz patted Sadie's arm, then looked at Jackson. "So what's our next move?"

"Patience," Jackson replied.

Sadie pouted. Liz hid a smile. If Sadie had her way, she'd be out there playing detective until she uncovered some kind of clue.

Jackson's gaze circled the room, stopping when he glimpsed the lone Amish person in the crowd. "Philip, thank you for coming."

Philip merely nodded.

Liz had been surprised by his presence, since the Amish dealt with troubles their own way within their own community. Had Jackson encouraged him to attend because his tools had been stolen when Philip had been at Cross Furniture? Or was the sheer gall of the thief enough for Philip to side with the townsfolk?

"Any other questions?"

Voices rose in a cacophony as people spoke over each other. Jackson held up his hand, looking like he was fighting a headache. Once he had the room quiet again, the door opened and Chief Houghton walked in. The barrage of questions started all over.

"Are town meetings always like this?" Liz asked, having to raise her voice over the din, even though Mary Ann sat right next to her.

"Only when there are major issues to discuss. Pleasant Creek residents like to be heard."

The chief held up both hands. "Whoa there, folks. Simmer down."

Within seconds the anxious chatter subsided. Even without answers, the inherent authority of the police chief standing in their midst was reassuring.

"I have my officers scouring the town and outlying areas. We've had a few calls about your belongings, but nothing concrete just yet."

"Who would do such a thing?" the town librarian asked.

"That's what I'm going to find out," the chief said, his tone determined in spite of the daunting task ahead.

"I've asked my assistant, Scott, to start a phone tree," Jackson went on to say. "He'll call or text with any news. Please make sure we have your most current contact information. Until then, know that we are doing everything in our power to solve this problem."

Voices rose again as the group gathered their belongings and stood to leave. Liz draped her purse strap over her shoulder as the door opened. Scott popped his head in and motioned Jackson his way. He said a few hushed words and handed Jackson an envelope before closing the door.

"Hold on just a minute more, folks."

He pulled the chief aside and spoke softly. They both looked at the envelope Jackson held in his hand. Suddenly the room was quiet enough to hear a pin drop as everyone strained to listen in on the conversation. After a few terse words, the chief left. Jackson faced the crowd.

"Scott just handed me a letter we need to read. It seems to be from the thief."

The noise level escalated again. Questions bounced around the room. Liz stared at Jackson, eager to hear what the letter contained.

"The thief knew we were meeting about him and sent a letter?" Mary Ann asked.

"Pretty brazen, isn't it?" Liz responded.

Sadie rubbed her hands together in anticipation. "Maybe now we'll find out what is going on. I wonder if the thief is making any outrageous demands!"

Liz gently elbowed Sadie. "You don't have to look so excited," she said with a smile.

As Sadie winked, the peacock feather in her hat bobbled over her head. She had been accessorizing with a lot of feathers lately. "But I am."

Mary Ann chuckled and threw up her hands as if to say, "That's our Sadie."

Minutes later the chief returned with a pair of latex gloves. He handed them to Jackson, who quickly pulled them on and opened the envelope. Liz sank back down in her seat as she and the other business owners waited to hear the latest bit of intrigue.

Jackson extracted a single sheet from the envelope, unfolded it, and read it before holding it out for the chief to read.

"A bit dramatic, don't you think?" Sadie muttered under her breath.

Liz rubbed the chills dashing over her arms. "Not if the bad feeling I have is any indication."

The chief's face became an unreadable mask as he glanced at Jackson. He nodded in response to the silent question in Jackson's eyes.

Jackson's attention turned back to the group, his expression also under tight control. Liz tried to tamp down the rising sense of unease brought on by his inscrutable demeanor.

The mayor took a breath and read aloud. "This letter is to inform all concerned that the personal items taken from you are being held for ransom."

The room was engulfed in stunned silence.

"Ransom?" Sadie finally said. "I knew it."

Jackson continued. "The only way to have your property returned is to hold a reenactment of the original town charter signing. This must take place on the day we celebrate as Heritage Day."

Murmurs rippled across the room. Rob Carver furiously scribbled notes.

"I have given you time to get this event together. You have two choices. Fulfill my demand and your items will be returned. If there is no reenactment, the town will pay."

"This is shaping up to be our most interesting Heritage Day celebration yet," Sadie said in a loud whisper.

"This is your first and only notice. I am holding Mayor Jackson Cross and Chief Stan Houghton personally responsible for the outcome. You have been warned."

While the letter was off-putting, the thought that the thief was holding Jackson and the chief "personally responsible" spooked Liz. The two men exchanged concerned glances.

"Oh my," Sadie breathed.

"My thoughts exactly," Mary Ann said quietly.

"This is outrageous," the librarian spoke from across the table. "What on earth does he mean, 'the town will pay'?"

Liz wanted the answer to that question too. "While these demands might seem ridiculous," she reasoned, "the personal threat is serious. We can't wait it out to see if the thief carries out his intentions."

"But what if this is a bluff?" Rob called out.

"Folks, let's take a breath right now and try not to jump to conclusions," the chief urged, clearly attempting to restore some semblance of calm.

"Jackson, what do you think?" Sadie asked.

"Considering I have a target on my back, I'd like to go along with the demand. At most, it will be inconvenient to pull off. At best, it leads us to the person making the threats. Let's vote."

The decision was unanimous to follow the instructions in the ransom letter. Liz felt another chill race down her spine. It seemed that a black cloud now hovered over the Heritage Day celebration that had nothing to do with the weather.

4

Liz waited until the crowd dispersed and Jackson finished his conversation with Chief Houghton before she approached the weary mayor. His gaze distant, he blinked from whatever held his attention when Liz walked up to him.

"Liz. You're a welcome distraction."

"And probably a much needed one." The conference room was empty now but for the two of them. Jackson had somehow managed to find a mug of coffee, the rich scent lingering in the air as if he'd just poured a fresh cup. "That meeting was quite . . . tense," she said.

He laughed. "Other than the odd circumstances, it was very similar to our town forums. Lots of opinions."

"I get that. But what I don't like is the personal threat to you and the chief."

Jackson waved her back to the conference table. She sat, smoothing her navy slacks and straightening her sleeveless blue-and-white-striped blouse.

"Not the best way to start the day," Jackson agreed, his hazel eyes crinkling at the corners, "but I don't feel the need to run out and hire a bodyguard. Unless you're offering?"

"You should take this seriously."

"I most definitely will."

"Doesn't seem like it," she countered. She tried to stay miffed at his cavalier attitude, but the twinkle in his eye made her relax a degree. No wonder everyone loved the mayor. He had a way of shouldering responsibility with ease, even managing to find humor in a very serious situation.

"Liz, I appreciate your concern, but the chief and I can handle this."

"What happens if this person changes his mind? Decides to come after you even if the demands are met?"

"Liz, I've been taking care of myself for a long time."

She blew out a breath. "Sorry. I realize you're a grown man. I'm just worried for you."

"After all the times I've watched you sink knee-deep into one mystery or another, welcome to the club."

She sent him a sheepish grin. "There is that."

"I'll be fine. Now, what can I do for you?"

"Actually, the ransom demands and my current question go hand in hand."

He raised a brow.

"I'm still a little fuzzy on my role on Heritage Day."

"I meant to get back to you, but then the thefts started."

"Can you explain now?"

"Sure." He leaned back in the chair. "As you know, Heritage Day celebrates the founding fathers of Pleasant Creek who brought back the charter from the state capitol to establish Pleasant Creek as a town. Along the way home, the founders were ambushed."

"Ambushed? For a piece of paper?"

He chuckled. "No. For what the assailants thought might be in the wagon. Which was just three men. But they survived and were considered heroes."

"What did the robbers think might have been in the wagon?"

"Who knows? Tools? Money? Hard to say for sure, although rumor has it there was an iron date marker that was destined for the newly built courthouse, but it never materialized. Maybe it was stolen during the raid."

"Why would someone take a marker? It can't have been valuable."

"Again, rumor. I can't say."

"So, these events led to this becoming a town holiday?"

"Essentially. A few years later, the mayor established Heritage Day as an official holiday. We've carried the tradition forward ever since."

"And this happened in July?"

"No, June, but the mayor decided to tie the celebration to Independence Day."

"I suppose that makes sense. Mary Ann told me about the Tour of Homes. Is adding the inn to the tour what you had in mind when we bumped into each other at the coffee shop?"

He nodded. "We like to have some of the more significant landmarks open to the public that day. Throw in a little history, maybe some cookies, and the tourists are happy."

"Even though the Olde Mansion Inn doesn't have anything to do with the founding fathers?"

"It was built after the charter was established, but, like every historic event, ways to celebrate have changed over the years. Somewhere down the line, this tour idea started and became popular so we stuck with it. Plus, it brings in money for charity."

"A draw for tourists and support for a good cause. Clever."

He held up a photocopy of the letter that Scott had made after the meeting adjourned. "I've been going over the demand again. In light of the items taken, it seems like the thief has a grievance."

"Whoever it is has certainly caused an uproar."

The paper fluttered to the desktop when Jackson dropped it. He rubbed his temple. "Now I have to appoint someone to pull the reenactment together."

Noticing Jackson's gesture, she realized he was much more concerned than he let on. Liz hated to see him so disturbed, but she knew Jackson would do whatever he had to do to keep the town safe, even at personal risk.

"Why a reenactment? Was that part of the original celebration?"

"When the festival at Pleasant Creek became an annual event, it included a reenactment of the signing at the courthouse. It was held for years afterward."

"But somewhere along the line the tradition stopped?"

"Yes. I don't remember the signing ever being a part of recent celebrations. I never heard my parents mention it either."

"So what does acting it out prove now?"

"Your guess is as good as mine."

"Maybe it goes back to the original signing somehow?"

His gaze met hers. "Wait. The town council has been meeting to discuss refurbishing the current building markers that have aged over time. From there came the suggestion to make changes to the names of some of the older buildings around Pleasant Creek. Combine the new with the old. One of the merchants in town has been very vocal about modernizing the names, so we've addressed his proposal."

"And everyone is on board?"

"We haven't taken a final vote yet. If it passes, the idea would be to get the town involved in suggesting new names. Throughout the years the residents and merchants have been behind the Heritage Day celebration growing in size. They donate a lot of their time and materials at their own expense because it's always been good publicity for their businesses. We thought the excitement of something new would be good for the community."

"Do you think the thief is aware of the name changes and doesn't like it?"

"It makes sense. There aren't many families tied to the founding of Pleasant Creek left, but Thomas Sullivan is on the committee. So far he hasn't weighed in, so we're still working out the details."

Jackson sipped his coffee, then placed the mug on the table. When he looked at Liz, the fatigue lines fanning from the corners of his eyes were more pronounced than ever. "Liz, I'll be honest. At this late date, I don't know who I can find to take this on."

Pursing her lips, Liz considered the alternatives. Jackson was between a rock and a hard place. He needed to stage the reenactment for his own safety, but he was swamped with his own duties for the event. He needed help.

"How about I do some research about the original signing and put together a team to act it out. Would that help?"

Surprise, then relief, lit his features. "You'd take it on? Even though I've already committed you to the tour?"

"You know I love to dig up stuff. It can't be too difficult." She paused a moment and thought about the logistics. What did she know about planning a reenactment? "Could it?"

"Not if you have the right partner."

She swallowed. "You?"

"No. I was thinking about Bert Worth."

She suppressed her disappointment. "Right. He's the obvious choice."

Jackson tilted his head and a full-blown smile touched his lips. "Why, Liz Eckardt, did you want to team up with me?"

She knew he was only teasing but hated the warmth she felt spreading across her cheeks. She adopted her best flirtatious tone. "A girl can wish."

Jackson let out a deep, rich laugh. "Too bad I'm already busy."

Liz pulled her purse strap over her shoulder and stood. "Then I should be off to find Bert. Is he at his office?"

"Every day."

"Then I'll see you later." She turned on her heel to escape when Jackson's voice stopped her.

"Liz?"

She looked over her shoulder.

"Thanks."

"Just doing my part for the town."

It wasn't just the town Liz was doing it for, and she knew it.

————— \\\\\\\\\\\\\\\\\\\\\\\\\ —————

Minutes later, Liz stood in Pleasant Creek memorabilia central. Actually, it was the lobby of the ornate courthouse located in the middle of the town square, downstairs from the conference room where she'd left Jackson. Bert's project now dominated the space, rows of empty wood-and-glass display cases standing at the ready to hold Pleasant Creek's most prized artifacts. Her heels echoed as she walked across the marble floor and then down the hallway to Bert's office.

"My goodness, Bert," she said as she stood in the doorway of his overstocked work space. "Last time I was here, you'd just started this project and only had a few boxes."

Bert, an elderly man with glasses and a full head of fluffy gray hair, grinned back at her. He was dressed in a starched, button-down shirt, tie, and sharply creased slacks. "I'll admit I have a tendency to get carried away. Plus, recruiting help from the historical society added to the volume of donations."

Liz gingerly made her way into the maze of a room, her nose wrinkling at the faint musty scent of old boxes. "When does all this go out into the exhibit?"

"Monday. I'd been waiting for the display cases to arrive, and now that they're here, I can get busy."

"I saw them in the lobby." She glanced around. "You've taken on quite a task."

"Indeed. I made up charts showing the placement of the pieces in the cases." He nodded to a poster board covered with neat, detailed drawings tacked to the wall. "There has to be order, you know. I also made placards with the history of each piece. All I have to do is set up the entire collection before Heritage Day."

"Do you need help?"

"No," he said curtly, as if he didn't want anyone to infringe upon his duties. He caught himself and said, "As of right now, I have everything under control. Along with some surprises up my sleeve."

Liz imagined Bert wanted to lovingly place each historical object of the collection in the cases by himself. She couldn't blame him, due to the hours and care he'd put into the project.

"If you run out of time, maybe the Material Girls can lend a hand?"

"No need, my dear." From under his bushy brows, his steady gaze captured hers. "But I think perhaps you've come here for another reason?"

"Guilty." She looked around for a place to put her purse, then settled it on the cluttered desktop. "You most likely heard about the thefts around town?"

"Who hasn't? Quite the topic of conversation."

"I left a meeting with the victims a short while ago. Whoever took our things sent a ransom letter."

He blinked, clearly confused. "Come again?"

"The thief wants a reenactment of the original signing of the town charter in exchange for the return of our possessions."

"Hmm. Extreme."

"I volunteered to look up the history surrounding the charter and to gather details so we can present the reenactment as close as we can to what transpired at the signing."

Bert grinned, already deducing why she had stopped by. "And you'd like my expertise?"

"I desperately need it. Although my mother grew up here, and I have Amish relatives, I haven't lived in Pleasant Creek that long." She leaned her hip against the desk. "I understand the legal ramifications of a charter, but the actual events of that day are a mystery to me, not to mention the identities of the founding fathers themselves. I was hoping you could tell me more about them."

"It's a fascinating tale with an equally fascinating cast of characters. The town's first mayor had big ambitions. It seems he had a yen to secure his place in history." Bert opened a box near his elbow and produced a set of tarnished cuff links. "I found these at an estate sale. After careful research, I have traced them back to that first mayor."

"Why didn't the thief take them?" She moved in for a closer look, but Bert withdrew his hand, making a fist around the old cuff links.

"I certainly can't say, but they will be part of the centerpiece." Bert quickly dropped them back into the box. "Now, it would be my utmost pleasure to dig into the past with you."

Liz rubbed her hands together. "Where do we start?"

"How about with the original document?"

"Lead the way."

Bert shooed her out the door, locked it behind them, and led her back across the lobby to his former workplace, the public records department. Liz thanked her lucky stars that she had such a knowledgeable person on her side. If anyone would know where to look, it would be a retired records keeper for Pleasant Creek. "The important documents are stored here."

He pushed through a glass door, with the word "Records" stenciled in gold paint on the front, and waved to a woman behind the counter. They crossed to the far side of the room, stopping before a wide, wooden filing cabinet. Bert pulled out a shallow drawer where documents were laid out flat. On top was the charter, enclosed in a clear, protective covering.

"How old is this?" Liz asked.

Bert pointed to the top.

Liz whistled. "1896. Same year the courthouse was built."

"Correct. The town representatives, Leo Granger, James Sullivan, and Preston Oates, traveled to the Indiana State House in Indianapolis, to get the charter. Despite being ambushed when the wagon broke down on the way home, they delivered the document to Pleasant Creek safely."

"Jackson told me the story."

"The entire story?"

Liz chuckled. "Not if there's more to it than that, but I'm guessing you will."

"In a nutshell, the men held off an attack by robbers while James feverishly fixed the broken wagon wheel. They all made it back to town in one piece. In honor of their near-death experience, a big ceremony was planned to celebrate the signing of the document by the town founders. A few years later, it became an official town holiday."

"Was a reenactment required every year?"

"I believe it may have been done in those early years to honor the three men who went through great peril to deliver the document. But it wasn't required as far as I know."

Liz tried to organize her thoughts, but there was too much information floating about in her brain. "Is there any way I can get a copy of the charter? I can use it in the reenactment."

"Certainly. We have copies in the back room."

Bert hurried off to obtain her copy, leaving Liz to ponder. Even though the charter had come from the state government, obviously the founders were proud of the challenges they'd overcome to make Pleasant Creek an official town. And now, after more than a century, someone wanted the reenactment to be part of the Heritage Day celebrations once again, at an unnamed cost. Which meant she had to cover all her bases. She didn't want to endanger Jackson because she didn't do her research.

Bert returned minutes later, carrying a rolled-up document.

"This should do," he said as he handed it over.

"Thanks. Looks like I have homework in store for me tonight."

As they headed back to Bert's office so Liz could retrieve her purse, a thought occurred to her. "Bert, is there any chance that the town memorabilia you've collected includes stolen items?"

"Of course not." His bushy brows angled over his eyes for a moment before he quickly looked away. "Most folks think my love for history is an obsessive hobby, but they humor me. In fact, most people are happy to lend me family heirlooms and such, because they know me and trust that I'll honor and protect their valuables. Why would the thief steal from others then give the items to me? It doesn't make sense."

"This person went to great lengths to covertly abscond with our things. He could have stolen the items and then donated them to the exhibit in an effort to cover his tracks. Or he could have stolen things that had already been donated to you. Are you missing anything? I imagine you have a list of every piece in the exhibit, and the donors?"

"No, nothing is missing, and of course I have a list."

"The police will probably want a copy to compare the list of missing items against it."

"Good heavens. I hadn't thought . . ." His voice trailed off.

When they reached his office, Bert unlocked the door and scanned the room. "As you can see, this is far from Fort Knox. Anyone with a lock pick or even just brute force could have broken in and stolen all the items they wanted, but nothing appears to be missing. Why?"

Liz grabbed her purse. "I guess until the chief finds out who is behind this, we won't have an answer to that question."

Bert's gaze swept the room before he removed his glasses to clean them on his tie. "I must admit, I feel bad for the folks who had their belongings stolen, but I'm relieved nothing was taken from this room." His voice wavered. "This may seem like clutter to most people, but to me, it is hours and hours of collecting and painstaking research to discover the provenance of each piece. I would have been devastated if someone had run off with my work."

Liz patted him on the shoulder. "Thankfully, your collection seems to be intact."

Bert set his glasses back in place. "For now."

"I meant it when I said I'd help you find cheap labor."

"No thank you. I will finish this on my own."

Saying good-bye, Liz left the office. As she passed through the lobby, she couldn't wait to see Bert's plans and diagrams come to life in the display cases. Knowing his passion for antiques, it would be spectacular. Could that be why he seemed so territorial? Because of the long hours he'd dedicated to the project? The older man always lifted her spirits and, if all went well, he'd have the entire town smiling with pride over his time and effort to bring the past to life.

Stepping out into the noonday sun, the copy of the charter clutched in one hand, she noticed Jackson striding down the sidewalk before climbing into his truck. He started the engine and pulled away from the curb, heading in the direction of the police station. Her stomach did a flip at the thought of what might require Jackson to go to the police station in such a hurry.

Silly, Liz told herself. He could be going anywhere, like his furniture company, which was also in that direction. Jackson ran Cross Furniture in addition to his duties as town mayor. Still, the words from the letter haunted her. *I am holding Mayor Jackson Cross and Chief Stan Houghton personally responsible for the outcome. You have been warned.*

She shivered. The warmth of the day couldn't keep the worry from chilling her mood.

5

"Don't forget to visit the clock tower," Liz said after Saturday-morning breakfast. She chatted away, making sure her guests were pleased with their stays so far and giving them sightseeing recommendations. She cleaned up after they left the dining room before making her way to Sew Welcome.

A morning sewing class full of teenage girls had just ended. The chaotic blend of chatter, selfie-taking, and texting energized the store. Spying Mary Ann behind the register, Liz worked her way through the group.

"Good turnout," she commented.

"Summer is an excellent time for these classes. The kids need a constructive outlet, and their parents need an hour or so of teen-free drama."

Liz chuckled. "I remember those days. Goodness, were we ever as noisy as these girls?"

"I'm sure we were."

Soon the store began to clear out. Liz's voice returned to her normal register when she spoke again. "So Jackson finally explained the inn's role in the Heritage Day festivities."

"I did notice you hanging around after the meeting."

Liz looked anywhere but toward Mary Ann's perceptive gaze. "I wanted to know exactly what is required of me. As an innkeeper," she rushed to add. "I also committed myself to putting together the charter-signing reenactment."

Mary Ann's brows rose. "How did that happen?"

"Jackson is stressed out, especially now with the ransom letter and personal threat against him. I wanted to help. To be honest, now I'm curious about the origins of Heritage Day. And I'm hoping my research into it might provide some insight into the thief's motive, and buy some time for the chief if I can."

"Do you know anything about the origins of the charter?"

"Yes. Thanks to Bert. I stopped by his office at the courthouse to ask questions."

"If anyone knows the history, it's Bert," Sadie chimed in as she joined them. "He stopped here last week, asking for donations. This Heritage Day will be the first year to showcase his collection. I'm excited to see what he's gathered."

"The display cases arrived yesterday. That gives him two weeks to get ready." Liz thought back to Bert's somewhat overprotective attitude when she spoke to him. "Is he always so possessive?"

Sadie dropped spools of thread on the counter, righting one before it rolled off. "I suppose. He takes great pride in this town's history and his work to preserve it, and it's high time he got the chance to show off his knowledge."

Liz smiled. "He's so humble, though. So happy to share what he's learned through the years. Pride or no pride, he doesn't strike me as the type to do something like this for any special recognition. I only hope the new developments don't detract from his exhibit."

"You know," Mary Ann said, lowering her voice to keep the few customers from overhearing, "not that we could have known, but with everything we have going on this year, we probably should have made this a two-day event."

"We certainly didn't factor in a reenactment." Liz's shoulders rose. "Or the need to placate an elusive antiques-napper."

Sadie snorted. "At least he didn't take a person."

Liz shivered. "That would have been so much worse."

"We have to take this threat seriously," Mary Ann said, her voice firm. "Obviously, whatever is going on, this person is very upset and is willing to resort to theft and issuing threats to get his or her way. And having gone that far, there's no telling what else this person might do."

"Don't forget to add 'troubled' into the mix. This is not normal behavior." Liz sighed. "That's why I volunteered to get this reenactment organized."

"So where will you begin?"

"Bert gave me a copy of the charter, and I have a book about Pleasant Creek to read through. Since my guests are off sightseeing today, I thought I'd settle in and study. I need as much information surrounding the original celebration as I can find."

Sadie glanced at her business partner. "And I was hoping you'd mind the store today, Mary Ann. Many of the committees are holding last-minute meetings, and the historical society scheduled a get-together after lunch. My team is sorting through donations afterward."

Liz tilted her head. "Donations?"

"When Bert came up with the idea to display items pertaining to town history, the Pleasant Creek Historical Society sent out letters asking for donations."

"I didn't get a letter," Mary Ann said.

"I'm not in charge, so I don't know who got one. All I know is we agreed to help. Wanda Reese and Bert put together a list of people whose families have been here since the founding. We've handed some of the donations over to Bert, but have to sift through a few more."

Liz thought about the timing. The artifact drive by Bert. The thefts. A Heritage Day ransom demand. There was no way these events were unconnected. The question was, how to prove it?

"I can hold things together here. Go and have a good afternoon." Mary Ann turned to Liz. "And if you need any assistance with the reenactment, let me know."

"I will." A thought popped into Liz's head. "I'll probably need period costumes. Any idea where I can find any since it's so last minute?"

"The Pleasant Creek Playhouse has a wardrobe department," Sadie offered. "They recently hired a new director to take over operations when they reopen. Her name is Amber Pierce. You've met her, right?"

"No I haven't."

"She's been here in the store a few times. Each time she gives us details about reopening the playhouse, upcoming productions, and questions about how to attract donors. I thought you'd crossed paths."

"She likes to visit and fill us in on her life," Mary Ann added. "Since settling in Pleasant Creek, her husband has retired and plays golf daily. Reopening the playhouse and working part-time in the bookstore have given her purpose."

"Good to know." Liz came up with another thought. "Do you think she'd connect me with any actors willing to take part in the reenactment?"

"Actors are always looking for the next show. You can call and ask."

Mary Ann chuckled. "Need anything else?"

"Probably. I'll let you know when I figure this out." Liz looked around for something to write on. "I should start a list."

Mary Ann held out a pad of paper and pen.

"Always prepared?"

"Just like a scout."

As Liz jotted notes, shoppers wandered in, followed by the postal carrier, Max. He dumped a stack of mail held together by a thick rubber band on the counter, spoke to Sadie, and waved to Mary Ann, who had crossed the room to help customers.

"Left yours on your front desk," Max told Liz before leaving.

"I love getting mail." Sadie practically danced across the room. "You never know what surprises you'll receive."

"All I ever seem to get are bills and junk," Liz said.

Sadie waved a hand. "It's all about perspective. Think of it as an adventure. Each piece of mail is like an individually wrapped surprise you get to open and decide what to do with. Unless it's a bill . . . then I suppose you don't have much choice." She picked up the stack and began to sort through the envelopes. Suddenly she stopped. The color fled from her face.

Liz didn't like her unhealthy pallor. She rushed to her friend's side. "Sadie, what's wrong?"

With trembling fingers, Sadie picked one envelope out of the lot and held it out to Liz. The envelope was addressed to Sadie at Sew Welcome. Not unusual. The big "X" in bloodred ink across the front, however, was anything but ordinary.

"What in the—" Liz took it from Sadie's slack fingers. The name and address were printed on a label and affixed to the envelope. There was no return address. The thick red crisscross had been dashed over the envelope in a heavy hand.

Liz flipped it over. The back was blank.

Picking up on trouble, Mary Ann hurried over. Her eyes went wide when she viewed the envelope. "This is definitely not the kind of mail we normally receive."

"No one does." Liz handed the envelope back to Sadie. "Don't open it, and set it down so we don't add any more of our own fingerprints. I'll see if I can catch Max and ask him what he knows about this."

Liz raced out of the store, heading straight to the front door. When she stepped onto the porch, she saw Max moving down the sidewalk in the direction of the bakery. She set off in a hasty jog.

"Max. Hold up."

The man stopped and turned. "Something wrong, Liz?"

"Did you notice the heavy red 'X' across the letter addressed to Sadie?"

He frowned. "I didn't sort today. It was done before I clocked in."

"Does the office ever mark up mail?"

"No. If there's a problem with the delivery address I handle it personally since I know every person on my route." He swallowed. "Is Sadie okay?"

"Spooked."

"I can ask back at the post office. Find out who sorted."

"Thanks. In light of what's been happening lately, I'm calling Chief Houghton. He'll want to look into this too."

"This doesn't sit well with me. If I'd seen it I would have checked into it before I started my route."

"I know. Thanks, Max."

Liz strode back to the inn. She didn't like this newest development. Not one little bit. By the time she returned to the store, Sadie had torn open the envelope and was reading a letter.

"Sadie. You should have waited until we called the chief."

"Not when I needed to know what's inside." She frowned. "This doesn't make any sense."

"What doesn't?" Mary Ann asked.

"This is a letter like the ones the historical society sent out asking for donations." She held up the generic form letter. "We left a space on top to write in names of those on the donor list. 'Dear . . .' You fill in the blank."

Liz looked closer. Where a name would have been penned in, Forgotten was written in big bold letters.

"As much as I hate to say this, it looks like the letter is from the thief."

Sadie shivered. Every one of her seventy-plus years showed on her face.

Mary Ann helped her to a chair. "Call the police," she called to Liz over her shoulder.

"Way ahead of you." Liz already had the phone in hand, hitting speed dial.

The chief showed up fifteen minutes later to collect the letter, not happy that Sadie had opened it, but resigned to the fact that no one could tell Sadie what to do. She was uncharacteristically subdued. They had to figure out what was going on soon. Liz wanted to see healthy color back in her friend's ashen cheeks.

Sadie placed a hand on Mary Ann's arm. "Call Wanda. Ask her to bring the master list here so we can look at it."

After finding the woman's number, Mary Ann placed the call. "Wanda promised to be right over," she reported after ending the conversation.

Liz paced the store. "This now makes three people who've been threatened. Maybe Heritage Day should be called off this year."

A hint of color tinged Sadie's pale face.

"No," she insisted. "We carry on. Liz, plan the reenactment. We must follow through."

Liz swallowed hard. There had to be some way she could shield her friends from the menacing mind games the thief was playing. "Maybe we—"

"No," Sadie cut her off. "This is our town. No one can make us afraid unless we let them."

Liz admired Sadie's principles but couldn't shake her own sense of helplessness.

Visibly upset, Mary Ann moved from her place beside Sadie. "I'm closing the store today." She marched to the counter and began to write a note in big letters on a blank piece of paper. "We'll place a sign out front alerting customers we'll open again on Monday."

"If we do, this person wins," Sadie argued.

"Or we get a few days to regroup," Liz countered.

Sadie crossed her arms over her chest. "Either way, I don't like it."

"Humor me." Mary Ann affixed tape to the paper and left the store.

"She's worried about you," Liz said in a quiet voice. "We all are."

"I've been taking care of myself for a long time, Liz. This is just a bump in the road."

"Gee, where have I heard that before? Oh yeah, from Jackson when I expressed concern over the threats made on his life."

"Jackson can more than take care of himself. He's smart. And I'm no dummy, either."

"But no one is invincible. Especially since we don't know where the threat is coming from."

"Then we'll just have to figure it out and keep our wits about us in the meantime," came Sadie's stubborn reply.

Liz blew out a breath.

Mary Ann returned, Wanda Reese trailing behind her. A retired elementary school teacher close to Sadie's age, Wanda wore her short white hair in a trendy style and designer glasses that highlighted her bright blue eyes. Her petite body was nearly dwarfed by the large tote bag she carried, which slapped against her leg as she walked.

"I just heard what happened." Wanda rushed to Sadie. "Are you okay?"

"It was just a letter. I'm fine."

Right, Liz thought. Sadie's still pale face belied her words.

Wanda dropped her tote on the floor. "This is very disturbing, I must say."

"That's why I wanted you to come by. We need to go over the list. Maybe you missed someone or left off a key donor. Someone who might have been offended by the oversight."

"I don't see how." Wanda pushed her glasses up the bridge of her nose. "I'm very organized."

"If you're referring to your organizational system which includes a disappearing file where important papers often end up, never to be seen again, then I beg to differ," Sadie said.

"That only happened a few times."

Sadie rolled her eyes.

"Okay, five." Wanda jammed her hands on her hips. "Finding people to join the society is getting harder all the time. None of the young people in town are interested, so members are overworked."

Sadie patted her friend's hand. "Sorry, Wanda. I didn't mean to sound ungrateful. I'm still reeling from the letter."

Wanda's indignation softened. "I understand." She picked up her tote again and rifled through the voluminous bag. "I have the list somewhere . . . Oh, here it is."

She pulled out a file folder and handed it to Sadie. Liz and Mary Ann moved in behind her to read over her shoulder.

Sadie ran her finger down the list of names, each matched with a corresponding check mark. "Does the check mean you mailed a letter?"

Wanda nodded.

"Some checks are missing."

"What? No. That can't be right. Give me that." Wanda took the paper and read. "Oh dear. It seems we did miss a few."

"We?"

Wanda looked everywhere but at Sadie. "Rosemarie and myself. I think we got our signals crossed."

Liz moved around Sadie. "How many names weren't checked off?"

Sadie took the list back, reviewing the names. "Mary Ann. George and Opal. They're . . . oh no."

"That doesn't sound good," Mary Ann said.

Sadie glanced up. "We somehow failed to send a letter to an important person. Lilith Granger."

"Who is?" Liz queried.

"A descendant of one of the men who brought the original charter to Pleasant Creek."

6

"So now what do we do?" Liz asked the uncomfortably silent room.

Sadie and Mary Ann exchanged uneasy glances.

A knot tightened in the pit of Liz's stomach. "Am I missing something?"

"Sadie and Lilith were once best friends," Mary Ann explained. "Handling this is going to be . . . tricky."

"I haven't seen Lilith in years." Sadie let out a long sigh. "She's going to take this personally."

She couldn't imagine Sadie having problems with anyone. She might be too opinionated for some people's tastes, but Liz knew Sadie was as kind and generous as she was outspoken. Whatever the cause of her falling out with Lilith, it must have been substantial if the uneasy looks were any indication. Liz gestured toward the list. "Personally enough to send threatening letters?"

"I doubt it. And I can't imagine her taking our belongings. First of all, why would she want them? Her ties to the charter are forever linked to the town. She has nothing to prove. And second, she's become something of a recluse. I don't think she gets out much."

"I see her from time to time," Mary Ann confessed. She colored at Sadie's sharp glance. "I just never mentioned it since you two are estranged."

"Maybe she recruited someone to work with her?" Liz threw into the mix.

Sadie bit her lip. "I can't see it."

"I'm sorry, Sadie. This is a colossal mix-up," Wanda admitted.

"Certainly it's one we can fix." Sadie rose and smoothed her skirt. "We'll have to go apologize for the perceived snub and let Lilith know it was nothing personal."

"Right now?" Liz asked.

"Better to take care of this before already hurt feelings turn bitter." Sadie looked at Mary Ann. "Would you drive?"

A knock on the door interrupted the conversation. Mary Ann hurried over to find five women standing outside in the rotunda. "We've driven a long way to shop here," one of them said irritably. "You didn't announce on your website that the store was closed today."

"I . . . we had a personal issue come up," Mary Ann explained.

"But it has been rectified," Sadie called across the room. "Please come in. The store has reopened."

Neither Liz nor Mary Ann could argue with Sadie without causing a scene. As Mary Ann ushered the shoppers in, Liz stopped Sadie in her tracks. "I'll drive you."

"You're busy," Sadie huffed.

"And you still look rattled. As long as we're back in time for coffee hour with my guests, I'm taking you to visit this person."

Sadie's scowl eased. "Thank you."

"What about me?" Wanda asked, hoisting her tote strap over her shoulder, nearly toppling under the size and weight of the bag.

"Go to the historical society meeting. Let the others know what has happened and tell them I'm handling it."

"Okay, but promise to call me later."

"I will," Sadie collected her purse. "Oh, Wanda, do you have an extra letter? I should give one to Lilith."

"Of course." It seemed to take Wanda forever to dig through her tote, but she finally came up with a slightly wrinkled letter.

"Excellent," Sadie said as she folded it to place in her purse. "Liz?"

"Right. Let me get my keys and we're off."

Minutes later, following Sadie's instructions, Liz drove through town. Sadie waved to friends they passed, but remained tight-lipped. Liz felt a pang of concern for her friend and wished there was something she could do to get Sadie back to her usual chatty self.

At the edge of town, Liz turned west and traveled five miles before turning onto a side road. The pavement, pitted and gouged by time and neglect, littered with large potholes, proved difficult to navigate. She winced when her Acura bottomed out at least three times and hoped her hubcaps would be intact after this rocky voyage.

Gripping the steering wheel, Liz maneuvered her car as though she were on an obstacle course. "The town should come out and repair this road."

"It's privately owned. The home owners have to cover the cost."

"Then they should get together and make arrangements to get it repaved. Aren't people afraid they'll ruin their cars?"

Sadie pointed ahead. "Lilith's house is the only one on this road."

As Liz drove closer, they topped a rise and a house came into view. Sadie fidgeted with her seat belt, the single action revealing her continued nervousness.

"Want to talk about what happened between you and your friend?"

"My goodness, it was so long ago now, I barely remember."

"I don't believe you."

From the corner of her eye, Liz saw Sadie stiffen.

"Come on," Liz continued. "You can recall childhood parties in vivid detail but you can't remember a friendship ending?"

Sadie stared out the passenger window. "It was long ago. Silly, really."

"But enough to keep you at odds?"

"Yes. I went on with my life, Lilith with hers."

They pulled up a long, dirt-packed driveway with scattered

pebbles leading to a two-story farmhouse. The closer they came, the more dilapidated the building appeared. White paint peeled in brittle curls. Faded green shutters hung haphazardly. Scraggly overgrown grass in the front yard spread into scattered brown patches, a testament to the overall neglect. A beat-up sedan, parked beside the house, listed on its axles.

"My goodness," Sadie said, shock in her tone, "this place is a wreck. Why on earth has Lilith let her home go?"

Liz stopped the car and turned off the ignition. Pings from the cooling engine cut the silence as they sat and observed the sad house.

"I'm guessing she lives alone?"

"Her husband died ten years back."

"Clearly she can't maintain this place by herself. Doesn't she have any children to help her?"

"They left Pleasant Creek years ago and as far as I know haven't been back." Sadie frowned. "Knowing Lilith, she hasn't told them the house needs repairs."

A curtain fluttered behind a window beside the front door, just as quickly falling back into place.

"I think your friend knows she has company."

Sadie opened the car door. "Brace yourself."

With those cryptic words, Liz exited the car, carefully making her way around the hood to join Sadie. Together they walked up the weed-infested, chipped-cement walkway to the front steps. Liz held out a hand to block Sadie.

"The wood doesn't look very sturdy. Let me test it first." Placing one foot on the bottom step, Liz applied some weight. The wood sagged and moaned, but held up. Feeling lucky, she made her way up the next two, gingerly working her way across the porch. She made it safely to the door, then turned to Sadie. "You should be safe."

Clutching her purse to her chest, Sadie cautiously climbed to the porch and joined Liz. Her finger wavered over the bell, then she stabbed the button.

Moments passed but nothing seemed to stir in the house.

"Where is she?" Liz moved to the window, cupping her hands around her eyes to peer inside. "I wasn't seeing things when the curtain moved."

"No, I saw it too," Sadie assured her. "This is Lilith making a point. She always had a flair for the dramatic."

Knowing that Sadie never wanted for flair herself, Liz couldn't imagine what Sadie considered over the top.

Impatient now, Liz rang the bell herself. This time she knocked on the faded door as well.

"She'll come when she's ready," Sadie said, clearly settling in to wait.

A breeze drifted by, mussing Liz's hair. She brushed the strands from her eyes and shifted her stance.

Finally, distant footsteps echoed from inside the house, growing louder as the occupant approached. After what sounded like five dead bolts being unlocked, the door opened just wide enough for Liz to see the woman inside. Silver hair pulled up into a messy bun on top of her head and a baggy dress covering her stout frame, the woman stared back at them. Her eyes sparked with recognition when she saw Sadie. Opening the door wider and pulling herself to full stature, Lilith's eyes narrowed.

"Sadie Schwarzentruber. I never thought I'd see the day you'd darken my doorstep."

"Lilith." Sadie nodded her greeting. "If you have a few moments, I'd like to speak to you."

"Not in this lifetime."

Lilith slammed the door shut with the strength of a twenty-year-old.

The entire frame shook under the force, making Liz jump and Sadie flinch.

"Wow," Liz muttered as she regarded the closed door. "You weren't kidding about the dramatic flair."

Sadie took the folded letter from her purse and wedged it between the door and the jamb. "Sadly, I wasn't."

––––––––––––––

As they made their way down the private road away from Lilith's house, Liz drove carefully out to the main road to avoid getting stuck in one of the numerous ruts they'd encountered on the drive in.

"I have an idea, while we're out," Sadie said once they were on the paved road.

After the unsettling run-in with Lilith, Liz couldn't imagine what her friend had in mind. "Which is?"

"After our less-than-successful attempt to placate Lilith, it's safe to say she won't be any help with the Heritage Day festivities. Let's stop by Thomas Sullivan's house. His ancestor fixed the wagon wheel on the trip back from the capitol. He might be able to add family details to your research."

"Any help I can get sounds good to me."

"His wife Claire stopped by Sew Welcome last week. Said they were going to stay home and relax on Heritage Day, but he might have some insight you won't get from only reading about the events."

This time Sadie directed Liz back into town, then east through a nicely maintained neighborhood. The lots were large enough for pool enclosures, stand-alone garages, or a shed in the rear of the property. At the end of the street, Sadie pointed out a ranch-style house, protected from the sun under the shady limbs of mature, leafy trees. The yard, a healthy green, mowed and neat, was bordered by a flower bed running the length of the house and boasting vibrant annuals. The driveway was empty, although the vintage truck inside the open garage indicated someone was home.

Liz pulled up and parked, waiting for Sadie's lead. Her friend just sat there.

"Sadie?"

Sadie shook her head. "Sorry. I can't get the vision of Lilith's home out of my mind."

"When was the last time you were out there?"

"Oh my. A good forty years ago."

The screened front door opened to reveal a barrel-chested man, dressed in denim overalls and red T-shirt. Tufts of white hair stuck out from under a ball cap. He closed the door behind him and crossed his beefy arms over his chest, waiting for the ladies to come forward.

"He seems a little more inviting." Liz knew her humor came off flat.

"That's just Thomas," Sadie chuckled as she exited the car.

Liz let Sadie lead the way. *This was her idea, after all.*

"Thomas," Sadie said. "Good to see you."

"Haven't seen you in forever, Sadie."

"I'm a busy woman."

"What can I do for you?"

"Actually, my friend here, Liz Eckardt, owner of the Olde Mansion Inn, is putting together a reenactment for Heritage Day about when your granddaddy brought the charter back to Pleasant Creek."

His eyes lit up. "Heard about all the trouble surrounding Heritage Day. I'd be happy to do my part. The Sullivans go way back. Bound to have some old family journals with stories about that day. I'll have to dig 'em up."

"I'm just beginning to look into it," Liz said. "Can I call you for details?"

"Sure can." He looked at Sadie. "Heard about the historical society donation drive. Claire donated a few odds and ends." He glanced at Liz again. "You're not from around here, are you? My family line goes back to the original blacksmith to settle in Pleasant Creek. He founded the Sullivan Ironworks. It's still up and running today." His tone was matter-of-fact.

"How interesting. It must be exciting to know your ancestor was one who brought the charter back to town."

"James Sullivan saved the day by fixing the broken axle on the wagon. He always had a knack with tools, or so the family story goes."

"You must be proud," Liz said.

He lifted a shoulder. In humility? "I have lots of information on the ironworks. Did you know the town was built on—?"

"Thomas," Sadie cut in, "this is about the family."

"The ironworks is the family business."

"Yes, but Heritage Day is about your ancestor."

"I don't see the difference."

Liz held up her hand. "Mr. Sullivan? Let me get my notes together and I'll call."

"Fine," he grumbled.

Not exactly the reaction she'd expected. It seemed he'd rather talk about the business than his family.

"Well then, Thomas. Thank you for your help," Sadie said.

Before they could leave, a woman with short, gray hair popped her head out the door. "Is everything all right?"

"Just telling these ladies about the Sullivan clan."

A tentative smile appeared on the other woman's lips when she glimpsed the women. "Sadie. How are you?"

"Just fine, Claire. You?"

"Well, thank you for asking. I was just about to—"

"They have to leave now," Thomas said.

"Oh, oh, I see," his wife stumbled over her words. "Sadie, we'll catch up another time."

Sadie opened her mouth to speak, but Thomas had already guided his wife inside and shut the door.

"Such interesting friends you have," Liz commented as they walked back to the car.

"Not really my friends, even though I grew up with both Lilith and Thomas."

"I hate to say it, but he puts the 'grumpy' in 'grumpy old man.'"

"He was the same at twelve."

When they were inside the car, Liz backed out of the driveway. "I don't know about you, but I could use an iced coffee. What do you say, Sadie? My treat."

"I'll take you up on that offer. This afternoon was tough."

Liz drove down Main, finding no parking spots available. She turned onto a side street just a few blocks from The Coffee Cup, a small diner. She parallel parked in the first open slot she found. "A walk will do us good," Liz said as she and Sadie stood on the sidewalk. "To work off the nervous energy."

"Sorry you had to witness Lilith's attitude today, but I rather expected her reaction."

"Let's put it out of our minds for now. There's nothing more you can do to change her response to the situation."

"At least Thomas wasn't completely opposed to helping us." Sadie frowned. "Even if he did get a little prickly there at the end of our visit."

"Thomas seems proud of his business."

"Sometimes it makes him a little hard to deal with."

From what she'd seen, Liz wouldn't argue with that.

Once inside the diner, Liz placed their orders. They visited with a few folks before Liz motioned to Sadie that she had to get going. Since Sarah wasn't working today, Liz had to ready the tea and cookies for her guests.

"So what's next?" Liz asked as they walked to her Acura.

"Next week I'll visit Lilith again. I'll bring Mary Ann along for support. She has a way of smoothing over a situation."

They turned the corner, but as they neared the car, Liz slowed. "What is that?"

She tilted her head as she walked to the front of the car to find something white fluttering against her tire. Was it debris that had blown down the sidewalk? As she crouched down beside the front wheel, she sucked in a breath.

Sadie hovered behind her. "What is it?"

The white object was one of the historical-society letters that Wanda had mailed to potential donors. A small knife plunged through the letter and cut right into the tire.

7

After calling Mary Ann to come pick up Sadie, Liz stood beside the car as Officer Gerst took her statement. The knife, an antique with a yellowed ivory hilt, and the historical society letter had already been bagged as evidence. The threat was primitive, but effective.

"You were only away from the car for fifteen minutes?"

"Tops."

"And you didn't see anyone hanging around?"

"No."

Along the block where Liz had parked were professional offices, all closed on a Saturday afternoon. There was no chance of an eyewitness unless a tourist happened by.

The technician who had dusted her car for prints closed his case, gathered the bags of evidence and, with a nod, strode back to the police station.

Watching Officer Gerst taking notes, she asked, "Can I call Jake's Automotive now?"

"Sure." He closed his notepad. For a young man, he took notes old school. Liz found it endearing. "We'll let you know if we discover anything."

Liz pulled out her phone.

"Are you going to be okay, Miss Eckardt?"

"Yes. As soon as Jake gets here, I'll be on my way home."

"You don't need to call Jake."

Liz spun around to see Jackson, his long-legged stride leading him her way, a frown marring his handsome face. His work truck was parked a few spots down from hers.

"Jackson. What are you doing here?"

"The chief called. He's keeping me informed of any new developments." He glanced at her car. "This qualifies."

She was thankful he cared, but, like Sadie and the Borkholders, Liz liked to handle her troubles on her own. "It's under control."

Jackson nodded to Officer Gerst, who tipped his hat and took off toward the station.

"Pop the trunk."

"Jackson . . ."

"Don't argue, Liz. I'm here and I'll change your tire."

"What makes you think I can't change the tire?"

He sent her a skeptical grin and placed his hands on his hips. "Go for it."

Liz exhaled sharply. "Fine. I don't change tires. Happy?"

"The first step to acceptance is admitting you have a problem."

"Changing tires?"

"Stubbornness."

She aimed her key fob at the trunk and pressed a button. The trunk lid swung up.

"Now was that so hard?"

"You do realize I'm more than capable of taking care of myself."

"I never said you weren't. I just figured after finding a knife in your tire, you might want some moral support."

"Sorry. You're right. I'm a little wigged out at the moment." She felt bad for snapping at him. This wasn't his fault.

Jackson uncovered the spare and pulled out the tire. He lowered it to the ground where it bounced before he rolled it to the front of the car. Next he found the jack and went to work.

"We could turn this into a teachable moment."

"You're going to teach me how to change a tire?" Liz shrugged.

"In Boston I always called a service if I needed assistance, but I'm not opposed to learning a new skill."

"You don't need to be an expert, but it couldn't hurt to watch in case you're ever in a circumstance where you actually have to do this yourself."

"Okay." She closed in, watching the process as Jackson's capable hands took care of her flat tire.

He looked over the punctured tire when he was finished. "I'll get this to Jake's. Looks too deep for a patch, but you never know. In the meantime, make sure you call the shop for a replacement."

"I will." She paused after examining the gash in the rubber. "This is getting out of hand. Thefts and letter threats are one thing, but whoever is angry about Heritage Day has crossed a line."

"I agree. Hopefully the chief will get some clues from the knife, or from the letter that Sadie got today," Jackson said. "On a related topic, I have news."

"Good or bad?"

"Depends. The chief picked up the inventory of Bert's collection. We were surprised the cuff links that Bert thinks belonged to the mayor at the time of the first charter celebration weren't stolen as well. Bert said his system would make it hard for anyone to find a piece that specific."

Convenient excuse? "I've seen his office. He's right, there's no way anyone would know where he stored the cuff links. Apparently, only Bert understands his system of organized chaos." She hated to think that kind, careful Bert could have a role in all of this. But his guarded behavior and the fact that he somehow avoided the thief's reach was suspicious. "What does the chief think?"

"Right now, he's collecting information related to the case, but he did say Bert wasn't happy to have his reputation under scrutiny. We'll have to wait and see what conclusion the chief comes up with."

"Let's hope for the best." Liz opened the car door.

Jackson stopped her by placing his hand on her arm. "Be careful."

"I could say the same for you. You were threatened, not me."

One brow rose.

"I don't think this was a warning for me," Liz said. "Sadie is the one involved with the historical society. The fact that we happened to be together this afternoon is the reason this person left their calling card pinned to my tire."

"You can't be sure."

"No, but it makes sense. I don't have any personal ties to town history. The English side of the community, anyway. All of you do."

Jackson nodded. "Good point."

"So I can be more objective about the details."

"What are you going to do?"

"First, I'm going to get the Material Girls together and talk about how we can ensure Sadie's safety. Then, I'll keep researching the charter signing like I volunteered to do. Maybe I'll uncover something new that will give us some answers."

"Thanks, Liz."

"Don't thank me until I have some concrete facts."

———————

"I think you know why I called you here for an emergency meeting," Liz said when the inn guests had left after coffee hour.

The Material Girls were assembled in her cozy sitting room, which Liz always thought of as the heart of the inn. The comfortable furniture, large fireplace along one wall, and crystal chandelier made this room a preferred gathering place for guests and friends alike. She'd served drinks and put out cookies, but no one, not even Sadie, had taken a gingersnap from the decorative dish.

Opal glanced at Sadie. "We're concerned about you."

Sadie remained as silent as she had since the other women had arrived, a mutinous pout on her lips, arms crossed tightly over her chest.

"You'd be the first one to protect us," Naomi said in her gentle way. "How can you expect us to react any differently?"

The reasoning seemed to penetrate Sadie's obstinate glare. Her arms lowered and she clasped her hands together in her lap. "I don't like being needy."

"You are far from needy," Caitlyn assured her. "You are one of the strongest women I know."

"But even strong women should know when to use good sense," Mary Ann added, then squared her shoulders. "We believe that knife in Liz's tire was a message directed at you."

"That's crazy. Everyone loves me," Sadie said, even if the uncertainty in her tone cast doubt on the statement.

"I can't imagine Lilith doing such a thing," Opal said, a frown wrinkling her brow. "Who else did you upset today?"

Sadie slumped down in her seat, looking dejected.

"Sorry." Opal's face colored. "I didn't mean it to come out like that."

"It's the truth," Sadie said.

Beans wandered into the room, his heavy girth swaying as he plodded along. He plopped down at Liz's feet and lay there, immobile. Absently scratching behind his ear, Liz said, "So tell us about Lilith. What happened between you two?"

Sadie took a sip of her tea and settled back in the armchair Liz had tucked her into earlier. "We were great friends in high school. Studied together. Stopped at Bontrager's after school for malted shakes." She picked at a speck of lint on her skirt. "We were in each other's wedding party."

"That's what friends do," Naomi said.

"Lilith had always been involved in drama productions in high school. So when the Pleasant Creek Playhouse opened its doors, she was excited to have a place to act after we'd graduated." A faint smile tipped her lips upward. "She had dreams of the bright lights of Broadway."

"She was that good?" Caitlyn asked.

"Oh heavens no. But no one wanted to break her heart with the truth." Sadie laughed. "She loved the theater so much, we humored her."

"So she did act?" Caitlyn continued.

"Oh yes. Sometimes she got the lead, but mostly she was a stand-in." Sadie waved a hand. "The Pleasant Creek Playhouse wasn't as famous as the Great White Way, but our reputation wasn't shabby either. Most weekends we had a full house. Folks from all over the county would come out to be entertained.

"After she'd been at it a few years, she nagged me into trying out for a part in a new production. I'd been helping with the costumes, but Lilith wanted us to star together. So I decided, why not? It might be fun."

Caitlyn was the first to slide a cookie from the dish. "What was the play?"

Sadie chuckled. "*The Taming of the Shrew.* I'm not a big Shakespeare fan, but Lilith hoped we would get the leads, Katherine and Bianca. We tried out and waited to see what would happen."

"Did you get a part?" Caitlyn asked.

"Yes. Katherine. Quite a coup for my first audition."

Opal leaned in. "And Lilith?"

Sadie sighed. "Understudy for Bianca."

"Oh no," Mary Ann muttered.

"Lilith was furious. Accused me of stealing a main role away from her on purpose. I offered to step down. I hadn't cared about the part either way, which made her even more distressed. She thought I pitied her. 'Acting is my life!' Lilith screeched at me." Sadie shook her head. "It was very ugly."

"Let me guess," Liz said. "You walked away from the role."

"Yes. But Lilith never spoke to me again. She continued to act, but over time her roles became fewer and farther between."

"How sad to let something like that come between you." Naomi wiped her eyes. "I just hate hearing about friendships ending over silly misunderstandings."

Sadie picked up her glass, but paused to speak before taking a drink. "Problem was, Lilith didn't think it was silly. I tried to make amends. I called her. Stopped by her house. I even tried to get her husband to intervene, but she was convinced I'd ruined her chance at the big time." Sorrow glistened in Sadie's blue eyes. She set the glass aside. "Our last meeting was awful. We said things we'll never be able to take back. Now that we're older, with a lifetime of memories to look back on, I'll always regret not trying harder to bridge the gap."

Naomi reached over and took Sadie's hand in hers. "It's never too late."

Sadie's chin lifted. "I just don't see how we could reconcile after all this time."

The room was silent for a long moment.

"I only ever wanted to sew costumes and make props," Sadie said, her normally steady voice quivering.

"Of course you did," Caitlyn said. "You do love drama, but you express it in your flair for clothing, not acting. If your friend hadn't asked you to audition, I'm sure you would have been completely happy sewing costumes."

"And hats," Sadie said, a bit of her smile returning. "The first play I helped with called for fancy hats to be worn by the actresses. I made the most divine hats and fell in love with them. After the production, I took them home and wore them out in public."

"I always wondered where your hat obsession came from." Opal smiled. "No one can deny your panache, my friend."

"I do know how to pick stylish apparel, if I do say so myself." Sadie laughed, at ease for the first time since the conversation started. "And now my knack for style translates to sewing quilts. I enjoy the challenge of coming up with original designs. Costumes were fun, but it was nothing compared to my love of quilting."

Opal clasped her hands together. "We agree with that statement. Your quilting talent, along with Mary Ann's, is what has made Sew Welcome so successful."

Sadie's good mood vanished. "I wish the same could be said for Lilith's passion. I'm afraid it's only brought her bitterness and hardship."

Beans stirred, having been awakened by Sadie's strident tone. He stared up at Liz, his big round bulldog eyes begging for food. "You'd think I never feed you," Liz griped to the more-than-spoiled dog. "Come on. Let's see what I can find for you in the kitchen." Liz rose. "Keep visiting," she told her friends. "I'll be right back."

Liz made for the kitchen. Beans's waddle was uncommonly fast as he followed. She scooped a small portion from his kibble bag and emptied it into his bowl. He stared at it a moment, then back at her as if to say, "That's it?"

She scratched him again. "That's all you get tonight, buddy. Enjoy."

He lowered his head and dug in. After replacing the scoop inside the bag, Liz washed her hands, turning to find Mary Ann entering the kitchen.

"Do you need something?" Liz asked from her place at the sink. "Cookies. More tea?"

"There's only one cookie gone from the tray. After Sadie's story, and what happened today, I don't think the ladies have much of an appetite."

Liz grabbed a towel to dry her hands. "Did you know the history behind Sadie and Lilith's acrimony?"

"Only that they both had connections to the playhouse. Sadie never told me the entire story."

"Do you think Sadie's right? That there's no chance at a reconciliation?"

Mary Ann shrugged. "I can't say. I pass Lilith from time to time in town. She seems pleasant enough, but if the hurt is as deep and has festered as long as Sadie says, we can't be sure."

"Promise me we'll never let anything come between our friendship," Liz said, replacing the towel on the rack.

"I can't see that happening."

"I'd bet Sadie and Lilith never did either."

Mary Ann didn't reply, apparently deep in thought.

"I love being here in Pleasant Creek," Liz said, her voice thick with emotion, "and I can never express how grateful I am that you took me in as one of the Material Girls. I can't imagine ever losing this."

"You won't. We have busy, diverse lives, but we stick together through thick and thin. I can't see any of our friends cutting ties for petty, jealous reasons." Mary Ann paused. "Lilith may have thought she had what it took to become famous. None of us here is looking to become a star or outdo one another in our careers. I'd say we're happy doing exactly what we're doing, and we support each other in all things."

"I agree. It seems a waste for the two of them to be estranged. You'd think that Lilith would want all the friends she can get at her age. A knife through a tire isn't the best way to go about making amends though."

"Do you think it was Lilith? That she might try to hurt Sadie?"

Liz held back a shiver at Mary Ann's last question. After having a door slammed in their faces and hearing Sadie's history with the woman, Liz wondered what Lilith was capable of. "You didn't see the look on her face when we stopped by her house. There's a lot of resentment stored up in that woman."

"She's an older woman who rarely leaves her house. What could she possibly do?"

"Work in cahoots with the thief?"

"I suppose we can't rule that out."

"I have an idea about Sadie," Liz said. "It might work short term."

"What do you suggest?"

"Sadie would never let one of us stay with her until this mess gets straightened out, but we can stop by at different times when she is home. I'm sure the girls will agree. In the meantime, I am going to call the chief. I'll explain what happened out at Lilith's and ask him to have a patrol car make regular swings by Sadie's house. For now, that's the most we can probably get away with without Sadie causing a ruckus."

Mary Ann ran her hands up and down her arms. "I hate the idea of her in that big farmhouse all alone."

"At least she keeps a loaded gun handy."

The color leeched from Mary Ann's face. "I hope she never has to use it."

8

Once Liz had secretly secured promises from the other Material Girls to check in on Sadie when she wasn't working at Sew Welcome, and her weekend guests had checked out, Liz had time to resume her study of Pleasant Creek history.

She'd stopped by the library and the lovely librarian had pointed Liz toward additional books about Pleasant Creek history. So far she'd learned that besides the fact that the courthouse was opened the same year, there were no specific references to the actual signing celebration.

Frustrated, she blew out a breath. Her best bet was to head down to the courthouse and question Bert again. The retired records keeper would steer her in the right direction.

"Sarah, I'm headed out," Liz called up the stairs. Her young employee had a list to keep her busy that morning. "I'll check in later to make sure you're okay."

A black *Kapp* appeared over the upstairs railing as Sarah looked down. "I will be fine. *Dänka.*"

Making sure she had a pen and a notebook tucked into a tote bag, Liz tossed her wallet and cell phone inside and headed out. Dressed in a soft pink top, white capris, and comfortable sandals, she exited the front door to stroll downtown. Roses greeted her as she walked down the sidewalk of the inn. The sun shone brightly in the cloudless blue sky. Liz noticed a spike in the temperature from yesterday, a sure sign that the full summer heat would be upon them soon.

She stopped at the end of the driveway to admire her newly decorated home and business. With Sarah's help, she'd hung the bunting. The dizzy danglers spun in the light breeze, flashes of sunlight reflecting off the metallic shapes. On the Fourth, she'd anchor the small flags along the path leading to the porch. Satisfied that the inn was ready for the holiday, she continued her journey.

When she reached the lobby of the courthouse, her eyes took a moment to adjust to the dim interior. When her vision finally cleared, she saw some of the display cases had been filled. Liz stopped to read the neatly printed description cards, marveling over the eclectic items Bert had found or acquired through donations.

Hand tools, china, clothing, and even old journals lined the shelves. The town's past was well represented. Having grown up in Boston, a city steeped in history, Liz couldn't help but feel a kinship to the folks here in Pleasant Creek. Artifacts and the stories of where they came from had always intrigued Liz, and Bert's collection was no exception.

"Ah, my first visitor," Bert said from the opening to the hallway.

"I'm honored." She pointed to the case. "You have quite a diverse collection."

"All from a town of very interesting people." His smile was infectious as he crossed the room carrying a shallow box. "My fondest dream is now a reality."

"A lovely display."

"Exactly." He seemed about to say something else, then hesitated.

"What?" Liz urged.

He set the box on the glass top of an empty case. "It may sound funny, but I don't want the past forgotten. With so much interest in high-tech gadgets these days, I'm afraid the younger generation will lose interest in their history, where they came from." He swept his hand over the room to encompass the display cases. "It took all this learning to build up to the cell phones and electronic tablets we take for granted. It's up to people like us, who care, to save history. Oddly enough, for the sake of the future, I must protect our heritage."

"You alone? That's a tall order."

"Not only me, of course," he hastened to add. "The entire town. My hope is that children will come through this exhibit and ask questions. Maybe they'll experience the spark of discovery."

"I recently had a similar conversation with Wanda. She was lamenting the fact that they didn't have any younger people volunteering their time at the historical society."

"If I could mix digital display methods with historical artifacts, I'd solve my own concerns."

"Then you need to keep an eye out when visitors come through your exhibit. You might find a young person as excited about the objects as you are. Then you could recruit him or her."

"That's an excellent suggestion, Liz. I will do just that." Bert's eyes danced with merriment. "If I have enough townsfolk like you rallying around the collection, I'm hoping its reputation will continue to grow and will draw tourists for years to come. So, to what do I owe the pleasure of your company today?"

"You remember I told you I wanted to look up historical records about the original charter signing."

"Yes. I thought about it after you left the other day and have an idea where additional documents might be stored."

"Great, because I haven't gotten far on my own." Liz frowned. "I don't want to take you away from your work, so can you just give me a general idea where I should look?"

"No, my dear. It's best I lead the way." He placed a few more items in the case and waved Liz toward the records department.

Liz glanced at the clearly marked door. "I'm sure I could have found the office since you brought me here the other day."

"Ah, but where to go once you're inside is the tricky part."

They walked to the floor-to-ceiling shelves, passing shorter filing cabinets and a few empty tables. In a corner, Bert stopped to scan a shelf filled with storage boxes. He ran a finger over each one as he read the labels.

"This is odd."

"What is?"

"I could have sworn the research materials I was going to show you were stored back here."

"Good grief. Don't tell me the history thief has struck again."

"History thief?"

"I just came up with the name after looking at the display in the lobby." Liz felt her face warm.

Scowling now, Bert said, "I rather think the title fits."

"It might be a little theatrical, but with different names floating around—thief, ransomer—I might as well give this person a moniker of my own."

Bert placed his hands on his hips, indignant. "Well, the records are gone. These documents are irreplaceable."

"Gone or moved?"

"I couldn't say for sure. Normally records are left alone, but with all the thefts, it seems possible the history thief beat us here."

"Great. How am I going to get the details right for the reenactment if I don't know the facts? It's almost as if he or she wants us to fail. Could the thief mean for us to jump through hoops to prove some point?"

"I can't say. All I know is that this person is a step ahead of us, and has been from the beginning." Bert glanced at the spot where the files should have been, then back at Liz. "Let's go back to my office. I'll see if I can locate anything that might help you."

They walked back to Bert's inner sanctum, as she had come to think of it. There seemed to be a dent in the number of boxes he'd emptied out.

"It's a work in progress," Bert said as he rustled through a stack of papers on the desk. "And now I have to worry about my collection. Apparently nothing is safe."

Liz pulled her notebook from her tote. "While you look, maybe you can tell me what you know about the signing. All I've heard is that the men protected the document when they returned from the capitol, and later, Heritage Day became an annual celebration."

"That's it in a nutshell."

"Have you read any papers explaining the actual signing ceremony?"

A faraway look glazed Bert's eyes, and he tapped his chin with a finger. "I recall seeing that Rodger French, the first mayor after the town received the charter, was involved because the courthouse was also christened that day. I believe there was a potluck gathering afterward. When I was a boy there were parades, but I believe that was more for the Fourth of July celebrations. Some years we had a farmer's market."

"So, what you're saying is that there are no written details about that first celebration."

"As much as I enjoy researching history, I've never had a reason to study this particular event. It has changed and evolved over my lifetime, especially as the population has grown. I imagine you would get a different version from anyone you talk to."

"So I'm back to square one." She closed the notebook. "Now what?"

"Without that missing box of records, your only alternative

would be to see if there's anything stored at town hall that was never brought over here."

"Right." She tossed the notebook in the tote. "Then off I go."

"I'll keep looking," Bert promised.

Liz stepped from the courthouse into the blinding sun, nearly bumping into Jackson. He grabbed hold of her arm to steady her.

"Liz. What're you doing here?"

"I'm on a mission to find out about Pleasant Creek's humble beginnings so you get a historically correct reenactment."

"Right." His lips twitched. "I should have known. You are conscientious."

"And curious. I want to know why the history thief is so upset."

His brows rose.

She clarified. "That's my name for the person responsible for this strange ransom situation."

"So, what did you discover?"

"Nothing. Bert couldn't find the records. I was headed over to your building to see if someone had borrowed them."

"I don't recall anyone saying they were going to request the records. Did he check in the courthouse basement?"

"He didn't mention that option."

"At one point the town council had talked about moving some of the old records there since space was getting tight. They might not have told Bert."

"Then I'll go back in and check it out."

"Need a hand?"

"Are you kidding? Yes, I'd love the help. If Bert doesn't know where to look, it might take forever on my own." She hitched her shoulder toward the door. "Let's go."

Jackson opened the door, and they walked back into the cool air of the lobby. Liz followed Jackson as he steered a path deeper into the building.

"So, what brings you here today?" she asked him.

"I've taken on the task of removing the old historical markers on the buildings. For the refurbishing project I told you about. We're getting them cleaned and restored or, in some cases, replaced."

"Can't town maintenance do the job?"

"It's sort of a pet project."

"So the marker change. Who came up with that idea?"

"Business folks who want to capitalize on town history. The bronze has aged, making the wording hard to read."

"Had you planned to do this before the history thief struck?"

Jackson turned down a long hallway. "We had. The town has some funds set aside for Heritage Day, which is a required item in the town budget. We thought we'd use some to upgrade the signage. After the celebration, we're going to do a face-lift on the town hall. Maybe even rename it."

"You don't like the current name?"

"It's named after the Oates family, and there are no descendants left alive. We thought maybe we could decide on a name that incorporates the old along with the new."

They reached the basement door. An old skeleton key stuck out of the lock. He reached out and turned the metal key.

"Is this for real?" Liz asked.

"I'm afraid so. The historical society has been instrumental in keeping the courthouse as authentic as possible." Jackson moved down a stair and held the door out for her. "Watch your step."

"What does the council want to change the town hall's name to?" she asked as she crossed the threshold, returning to their earlier conversation.

Jackson navigated the stairs in front of him. "The proposal is to go from Oates Hall, which no one calls the building anyway, to Pleasant Creek Oates Hall."

Liz followed close behind, grateful for a whiff of Jackson's citrusy cologne. It was much better than the dank surroundings. "Jackson, that's not much different."

"It's a start. We thought about having the town residents suggest names. You know, hold a contest, reward the winner."

"Good, because you need help coming up with a better name."

"Like I said, we've just been discussing the proposal." He flipped a light switch at the bottom of the staircase, which illuminated the nearest section of the cavernous underground storage space. "This way."

"So what about the other families involved in the signing? Do they have town buildings named after them too?"

"Sullivan Courthouse. Granger Library."

"In the time I've lived here, I've never heard either of the official names. Everyone just says 'the courthouse' or 'the library.'"

"See the dilemma? Some of the older residents might remember the family names, but over time, the buildings have become generic. We want to revive interest in the founders and their contributions to the town we call home."

"Well, I have to applaud your attempts to keep the town history relevant. I think that's what makes Pleasant Creek so popular with the tourists. They come back year after year for that connection to bygone days."

"Don't forget the town residents. Most every business owner goes out of his or her way to be friendly and helpful. Personal. Lots of small town charm." He made his way down an aisle between shelves. "And with technology vying for our attention these days, it's nice to be able to take a leisurely stroll along Main Street. No rush. No hurry. People can visit. They can window-shop with no pressure. It brings people back to another time."

"That's one of the reasons I fell in love with Pleasant Creek. And the inn."

Jackson neared the end of the aisle, yanking the dangling chain connected to a light fixture directly overhead. Nothing happened. He tugged again. "Looks like I need to get maintenance down here."

"Where would the box be?"

"Right here beside . . ."

"Jackson?"

"The spot where I thought it would be is empty."

Liz rummaged around in her tote until she found her phone. She pressed the flashlight app and scanned the area. "Technology does come in handy now and then."

"You won't get any argument from me." He held out his hand. "Do you mind?"

"Be my guest." She handed him the phone and stepped back while Jackson aimed the light over the entire shelf.

"Either someone else is interested in those files or our ransom-demanding friend has struck again."

Liz ran a hand over her forehead. "This can't be happening."

He shone the light on the floor until they were back in the main walkway under better lighting, then handed the phone back to Liz. "Nothing. We'll just have to make do with what we know."

"Which varies depending on whom you speak to. Bert had a bunch of different ideas, which were different from what you told me about Heritage Day. I bet if I took a poll, I'd get as many different answers as there are people."

"It's the best we have right now."

As they drew closer to the stairs, Jackson gestured up. "You go ahead. I'll shut off the light down here once you're up the stairs."

Liz followed his instructions, then reached out to turn the doorknob. "Maybe I can check old newspaper articles too. I—"

"What's wrong?" Jackson said.

"The door won't open." She turned the knob again, one way then the other. "It seems to be locked."

"That can't be." When he reached around her, she moved up against the wall to give him room. He jiggled the knob, but the door still remained closed.

The hairs on the back of Liz's neck rose. She swallowed hard. "Does this happen often? You take a girl down to the records basement, and the door conveniently locks?"

"As much as a romantic interlude sounds like fun, I never take women down here, and I certainly don't want to be locked in." He banged on the door. "I don't like this."

Liz pounded with him. After a few moments it became apparent that no one was coming to their aid.

"Now what?" She checked her cell phone. No service.

"Let's switch places."

Liz moved down the staircase, giving Jackson room. He rammed his shoulder against the door.

"Jackson! You'll hurt yourself."

"If I do this a few times, maybe the frame will splinter."

"Or your shoulder."

"Then I'll just use the other one." He shot her a playful grin.

"You joke now, but you won't be laughing when your arm is in a sling. Please be careful. We're in enough of a tight spot without you being injured."

He tried to force open the door two more times, but it proved to be a tougher opponent than he'd anticipated. He slumped against the wall. "Any other ideas?"

"We could go back downstairs and find something to ram against the door."

"Good idea."

"Wait." She stopped him by placing her hand on his arm. "What if whoever took the box is still down here? Maybe the locked door is a trap."

Jackson's muscles went taut under her grip. He held out his hand. "Your phone."

She reached into her bag, handing him the cell phone with shaking fingers.

"Stay here."

He hurried down the steps, flipping the switch at the bottom. Jackson swiftly made a visual sweep of the area, turning on the cell phone's flashlight app when he disappeared deeper into the darkness, out of her sight. Liz ran her hands up and down her arms to control a shiver.

Soon, he returned, climbing the steps to join her. "Clear."

She blew out a breath, dropping her phone in her bag.

"Come on."

They went back down, Jackson rubbing his shoulder as he went. He caught Liz's gaze as she watched him favor his arm. "Not a word."

She twisted an invisible key in front of her lips and pretended to toss it away.

"Look for something to pry open the door," he suggested.

"Like what?"

"A screwdriver. A flat piece of metal. Something we can slide in the crack between the door and frame to use as a lever."

Moments later she located a snow shovel and carried it to him.

He stared at her. "Really?"

"You wanted flat. This has a flat edge."

Shaking his head, he said, "I guess it's worth a try."

Jackson hefted the shovel and they climbed the stairs again.

"Let's try to slide it between the knob and the frame. Then put pressure on it. On three," Jackson said. "One, two—"

Before he could finish the countdown, a voice came from the other side of the door.

"Is someone down there?"

"Yes!" Liz and Jackson shouted in unison.

"The door is locked," Jackson yelled. "Unlock it from your side."

"The key is missing." The voice sounded like Bert. "Let me get help."

"I'd better hold onto the shovel until we know for sure someone can get the door open."

Minutes later, the sounds of bickering voices filtered in from the other side. Finally the knob jiggled, then strained as if someone was pulling on it, and the door popped open. In the flood of bright light stood Bert, his fluffy hair a halo around his head, blinking as he looked down at the shovel still clutched in Liz's hands. "That doesn't resemble a box of records."

An uneasy feeling washed over Liz. "How did you know we were looking for the records?" Liz asked. "When I left I told you I was going to check town hall."

"I . . . uh . . . thought I heard voices and came to investigate."

Bert's visible discomfort unnerved Liz. There was no way Bert could have known she and Jackson were trapped in the basement, so he must have been on his way down there for another reason, a reason he wasn't willing to share. And the look on his face when he'd seen Liz was holding a shovel instead of the missing records box—had that been . . . relief? Or was he simply nonplussed? Was it possible Bert knew more than he was letting on?

Hiding her suspicions until she could talk to Jackson in private, she lightened her tone. "Good thing. Otherwise we might have been stuck here a while."

"Plus, the history thief seems to have beaten us to the records," Jackson said, his expression grave. "And possibly even locked us down here."

9

"There's no way Bert just happened upon us," Liz said after Bert made excuses to hurry off to another part of the courthouse.

"You think he trapped us?"

"The timing does seem suspicious. Maybe he saw us come into the building and followed us."

"Why?"

"If he knew the box wasn't down there, he might have panicked."

"You think Bert took the box?"

"I don't know what to think."

Jackson seemed to mull over the conversation, then said, "I'll let the chief know what happened. Have him check out Bert more closely."

After insisting Jackson have his shoulder looked at, Liz went to the newspaper office. This was the only day she had to find any record of the signing before the holiday week rolled in. Time was running out. All the rooms at the inn were booked for the next two weeks, and with the town celebrations, free time would be almost nonexistent. She needed to make progress today.

Reaching the office of the *Pleasant Creek News & Views*, she pushed the glass door open and ventured inside. One phone rang while a reporter carried on a conversation on another line. The overhead fluorescent lights rivaled the sunshine outside. Desks and computers were scattered around the room.

The office manager, Marty, removed her glasses and closed up her notebook. "Hi, Liz. To what do we owe the pleasure?"

Before answering, Liz glanced around. She didn't see Rob Carver present and blew out a breath of relief. Liz and Rob didn't exactly see eye to eye, and she'd prefer to avoid dealing with the young reporter if possible.

"I'm hoping you can help me."

"What's up?"

"Do you have access to any articles that would have been written when the town was first settled?"

Marty's perceptive gaze sharpened at Liz's question. "We do have digital archives. Is there something in particular you're looking for?"

"Some details about the signing of the first town charter. And the first Heritage Day celebration."

"I knew it," Marty said. "Is this about the stolen belongings?"

"Yes, but—"

"I'm sure we can find what you need."

Marty hurried to her computer and typed on the keyboard. "We pride ourselves on keeping Pleasant Creek news available to the people, no matter the year published."

"Great." Liz lowered her tote and pulled out her notebook.

The other reporter in the office, Oliver, wandered over and leaned against a tall filing cabinet to watch as Marty pulled up the computer archives. "Those were the days. News reporters didn't have to go through so much red tape to request interviews."

"I don't know about town hall procedure," Liz hedged, "but I imagine this year's Heritage Day will give you plenty to write about."

"That's why an inside scoop would be awesome. Maybe you can—"

The front door flew open and a young man with red hair and freckles breezed in. *Great.* Liz had hoped to miss Rob, who had a tendency to sensationalize stories.

"What's going on?" Lifting the strap over his head, he dropped his messenger bag on the desk. "You guys get a lead?"

"Only if Liz here tells us what she knows," Marty said.

Rob came to stand beside Marty, looking over her shoulder at the screen. "The original Heritage Day?" He looked at Liz, excitement in his eyes. "So the mayor wrangled you into planning the reenactment?"

"There won't be a reenactment if I don't find out what happened on that day."

"Here we go," Marty adjusted her glasses on her nose. "June 25, 1896. Newly elected Mayor Rodger French stood on the steps of the courthouse to pronounce Pleasant Creek an official township." Marty's eyes moved as she skimmed the article. "A table was brought out front. A judge presided over the signing by the new mayor and the founding fathers, who brought the charter back from the State House. That's about it."

"Kind of disappointing," Liz said. Certainly not worth the trouble of issuing threats against the town or holding antiques for ransom. Or having to field Rob's questions. She recognized his dogged look. He wasn't going to let this go.

"Guess the people of Pleasant Creek kept things simple to honor the occasion," he said. She could sense the wheels turning in his mind, sorting out how to spin his next article.

"Well, at least I have an idea where to start." She jotted a few notes. "Can you print out a copy of this article and any others related to the charter?"

"Sure. Give me a few minutes." Marty typed in a few more commands. Before long, a large printer nearby whirred to life and rapidly spit out pages. "I'll also jot down the names of some other newspapers publishing at the time."

"Wait," Rob cut in. "Shouldn't we get an exclusive for helping you?"

"You can't consider this part of your civic duty?"

He looked at Liz as though she'd sprouted wings.

"Right. Well, I guess I'll be going then."

"Someone's got to figure out what's going on," Rob blurted. "I can help. I already have some leads. If we work together, we can figure out who the thief is."

Marty straightened and handed her the papers. Liz glanced down, pleased to see the articles were clear enough to read, despite the fuzzy resolution.

"He's got a point," Marty said. "We want a story, but we want answers too."

"The history thief isn't letting up," Liz said.

"The who?" Rob asked, sharp as ever when on the scent of a big story.

Liz waved her hand to brush off the comment. "Just my nickname for the person responsible for these thefts."

Rob grinned. "I like it." He hurried back to his desk and started typing.

Liz joined him. "You aren't going to use that name, are you?"

"Why not? It perfectly describes this guy."

"Won't it make him feel, I don't know, important? Like acknowledging him gives him liberty to keep on stealing? Rob, you were at the courthouse the day the mayor received the ransom letter. This person is dangerous and getting less predictable by the day."

"And if his crimes keep escalating, then we catch him." Rob's boyish grin made Liz's stomach turn. "It's a win-win."

Not if the other victims found out she'd not only dubbed the thief with a pet name, but had given it to the press to circulate. Would they think she wasn't taking the threats seriously? *I'd better leave now before I say anything else Rob can use against me.* "Thanks for the articles, Marty. I have to get this reenactment together and fast."

"Let me know if you need any help," Marty offered. At Liz's dubious look, she said, "As a citizen, not a reporter."

"You would do that?"

"Yes. I do have a life beyond the office."

Liz laughed. "I'll put you on the list."

Glad to be back outside, Liz patted her tote and yanked the strap over her shoulder. Maybe the other articles would shine some light on the charter signing. She'd traveled one block before noticing the Borkholders' flatbed wagon parked up ahead. Her first thought was of Miriam. Since the day the victims of the thefts had gathered at the courthouse, she hadn't had a chance to talk to her cousin and had wondered about her husband's stolen property.

Just before Liz reached the wagon, Philip exited the bookstore, Thomas Sullivan dogging his heels. Philip stopped and turned his back to Liz, but she could still see Thomas's animated face. Surprised by the anger she saw there, she stopped. Before she could process the scene, Thomas stomped away. Philip, his posture tense, shoved a large box onto the back of the wagon.

"Philip," Liz called out as she quickened her step. "Is everything okay?"

"*Hallo*, Liz." He nodded in greeting, but his eyes were hard to read. To others he might come across as distant, but Liz had spent enough time with the family to know that he was merely cautious. She couldn't fault him for that, especially in light of current events.

"Sorry you had to see that," Philip said, his voice clipped. A straw hat shadowed his face. "It was nothing."

"It didn't look like nothing."

As if knowing Liz wouldn't leave until she got an answer, Philip sighed. "It was a misunderstanding. I thought Thomas might know where my missing Werkzeugs . . . tools were."

"Why would he know?"

"In the past we have worked on projects here in town. He has borrowed them before. On a special job at his house." Philip frowned.

"He was not happy when I mentioned he might know the location of my stolen Werkzeugs."

"That explains why he stomped off."

"I misspoke. He has no knowledge of the thefts and was hurt that I accused him."

Liz glanced down the block as Thomas stepped up into his truck. She was about to ask another question, but Philip beat her to it.

"What are you doing in town?"

"Research. I volunteered to put together the reenactment the thief demanded so we can all get our belongings back."

Philip's eyes went dark. "You think it will work?"

"It's certainly worth a try." She shrugged. "It's not often the entire town gets a ransom demand."

"Many of the Werkzeugs taken from the wagon were in my family for generations. I would like to have them returned. I have always imagined passing these family possessions to Isaac. He is turning out to be a fine woodworker."

"I was curious the other day but didn't have a chance to ask. What tools were taken?"

"A carpentry wood plane, cabinet scraper, gouge chisel, and a draw knife. All were very well crafted, holding up much better than the new ones sold today."

"Miriam says you are very particular about your woodworking. I imagine these tools are priceless to you."

"To me and my family, *ja*."

"I know they're just things, but for most of us, the stolen pieces have emotional ties."

"I used them every day. If they are not returned, there is no way I can replace them."

"Were they taken right out of your toolbox?"

"Not my everyday box. I keep a special wooden container for the older items under the seat of the buggy."

"So it wasn't random? Someone would have known exactly where you keep them?"

He nodded. "I do not let the entire town know where I keep my antique Werkzeugs, but Thomas knows they were hidden under the seat. That is why I asked him if he knew anything."

"I only met Thomas the other day. Is he . . . pleasant to work with?"

A rare flicker of humor sparkled in Philip's eyes. "Why do you ask?"

"He seems to take great pride in his family business, Sullivan Ironworks. He wasn't interested in talking about much else."

Philip shrugged. "In the past we have talked about our shared interest in our family's history and heirlooms. Mine, and the old blacksmith pieces handed down from his ancestors. We are not friends, but we have a mutual respect for the care of the Werkzeugs handed down to us. He has quite an impressive collection himself."

"I wonder if the thief took any tools from him? He didn't say a word when Sadie and I stopped by his house."

"I could not say. But if so, he will want his belongings back too."

"Are there any other people you can think of who would know about your special tools?"

"I have worked with a few English through the years. These men have always been trustworthy." He frowned. "Or I thought they were."

"Then let's hope staging the reenactment works," Liz said. "Will you be in town for the celebration?"

"In the morning. I will set up the booth for Miriam and the others to sell their goods. I had not intended to stay."

"You might want to rethink your plans. Maybe hang around and see what happens when we meet the ransom demand."

"Perhaps I will." He glanced at the front of the wagon, and Liz sensed his urgency to be off.

"I'm sorry, Philip. I shouldn't have kept you."

"I finished building additional shelves at the bookstore and am headed home."

"Please tell Miriam I asked about her."

"I will. *Auf wiedersen*, Liz."

Philip untied the horse from the hitching post on the curb, leaped up onto the wagon seat and, with a snap of the reins, rolled down Main Street.

As she walked home, Liz pondered the scene she'd just witnessed. She was lucky to have gotten as much information out of Philip as she had. He was always very closemouthed. Her relationship with Miriam was likely the reason for Philip's transparency just now. That, or how upset he was over losing his family tools.

Thomas might not be willing or able to provide answers, but Philip was entitled to ask questions. And knowing Philip, he would never have started a conflict with Thomas without good reason. Had she overlooked something about Thomas?

As much as she'd love to know for sure, it would be impolite to press Philip for details. She doubted Thomas would discuss the conversation either.

As she drew closer to the inn, she saw a few of her guests on the porch. Glancing at her watch, she realized she'd spent too long away. She needed to get the afternoon treats served soon.

"Mr. and Mrs. Grayhill," she greeted, "did you have a good time in town?"

"Oh yes. Just as you said, Liz, the shopping was superb," Mrs. Grayhill said. "But Paul can't wait to tour outside of town tomorrow. He's eager to see the covered bridges we've heard about."

"I'm glad you're pleased," Liz said.

"But right now," Mr. Grayhill said, his cheeks red from the sun, "a tall glass of iced tea would hit the spot."

"Coming right up," Liz assured him. "You both enjoy the breeze, and I'll be back in no time."

"Oh, and Liz?"

"Yes?"

Mr. Grayhill grinned. "Would you mind bringing out the Amish molasses cookies, if you have any more? After tasting them yesterday, I can't stop thinking about them."

"They *are* good. I'll let you in on a secret." Liz scanned the front yard as if searching for hidden spies before lowering her voice. "I dream about them at night."

She hurried inside, first dropping her tote inside her quarters then getting the snack ready. The others guests would be arriving for coffee hour soon. Her questions about Thomas, Philip, and the history thief would have to wait.

10

Liz had just placed the last glass in the dishwasher and turned it on when a heavy knock came from the utility room door. Beans lifted his head but didn't leave his comfy spot. Grabbing a towel to dry her wet hands, she went to find out who might be visiting so late on a Monday evening.

She opened the door to find Rob Carver, a frown marring his boyish face. Behind him, the setting sun turned the sky a pinkish-gold, but the warmth of the day lingered. Freshly cut grass scented the evening air. Birds glided and dipped in the twilight sky. But she feared the delightful picture of a summer evening was about to be disrupted by the man standing on her doorstep.

"You didn't tell me everything," he accused.

"What do you mean?"

"Perhaps the part about the historical society forgetting to ask the founders' descendants for Heritage Day donations?"

"How on earth . . . ?"

"I have my sources."

Of course he does. "And your point is?"

He rummaged around in his bag to produce a copy of the historical society letter. "We can't solve the problem if I don't have all the facts."

"*We* aren't solving anything."

"Sure we are, if we work together."

Doesn't he understand how precarious this situation has become? "Rob, we are not the police."

He shrugged. "That doesn't mean I can't be part of the effort to find this guy."

She recognized the determined look on his face. Rob wasn't going anywhere until he got some answers. Opening the door wider, she motioned him in. "I just made a pot of coffee. Care for a cup?"

"Thanks," he said, following her into the kitchen and dropping his bag on the floor near Beans. The bulldog stirred, yawned, and then went back to his nap.

So much for fulfilling his role as a watchdog.

Liz poured two cups, then pulled a small pitcher of cream from the refrigerator and joined him at the center island. "Before we go any further, Rob, I want to know exactly what your motives are."

"A story."

"That's a given. Is there more?"

"Look, Liz, it's big news in town right now. Everywhere I go, people are talking. If I can get a scoop, it's major for my career."

"Are you planning to move to one of the bigger city newspapers?"

"If all goes well."

"See, that's what I'm worried about. The conflict of interest between advancing your career and making the best decisions for the town."

He blinked at her like she was speaking gibberish. "Can't I look out for both?"

"Not if it means spilling the beans and tipping off the culprit."

At the word "beans," the dog raised his head and barked.

"Not you," Liz said with a smile. Beans lowered his head again. "Look, I don't have a problem with you investigating a story. I just want to be sure you're keeping the town's best interests at heart."

"Fair enough." He reached for a packet of sweetener she'd placed beside the creamer, tore open the packet, poured it into the mug, and gave it a stir. "Full disclosure?" he asked.

"I'd appreciate it."

"You know I'm not going away. I need this story."

Liz didn't exactly trust Rob, but she understood his passion for journalism. "And what would you say if I ask that certain information stay off the record?"

He hesitated, fiddling with the spoon. "If that's your condition, yes."

"What do you want to know?" Liz said.

"Why was Mrs. Granger left off the list?"

"Clerical error. An honest mistake."

"So you don't think she'd retaliate?"

"Rob, don't you think people would notice if Lilith started showing up in the places our belongings went missing and put two and two together?"

"I don't know. From the folks I've talked to, I've learned that Mrs. Granger has been seen in many of the places hit by the thief."

"I just don't see it. Why would Lilith steal anything?"

"She's an odd old lady."

"That's not a strong motive to break the law."

"She's always seen carrying a large purse when she stops by some of the stores in town."

"Maybe she's just shopping. People like to engage in that pastime, you know."

He sent her a sour look. "I think there's more to it."

"Based on?"

"The fact that she frequents the shops where items were taken."

"So do I and many others. Do you have any proof that she's guilty?"

"No," he grumbled. As he took a sip of coffee, the conversation lagged a few moments.

"Has she been at every location where something was taken?" Liz questioned.

"Well, not that I've been able to substantiate."

"Then you don't know for sure she's the one behind the thefts."

"It makes sense."

"Why? Because the ladies at the historical society forgot to send her a letter? By that logic, you'd have to include Mary Ann, Opal and George, and anyone else they left off the list."

"It was a long shot." His shoulders slumped. "Any news about the knife in your tire?"

She held back a shiver. She'd reasoned that the knife wasn't meant for her, but what if she was wrong? It had been her car, and she had agreed to head the reenactment. "Not so far."

She glimpsed the disappointment in his eyes. He might be eager to rush headlong into a story that could launch the next phase of his career, but she had to remind him to use common sense. "It sounds like there are still a lot of pieces that need to fall into place. If you keep at this, I'm sure you'll uncover the truth."

Rob downed a final swallow of coffee and slid off the stool.

"I'll ask around again tomorrow. Maybe branch out to see if Mrs. Granger has stopped by other establishments."

Liz pictured the older woman's sad-looking car parked in her weedy driveway, her baggy dress, and angry eyes. She was not a woman who would go unnoticed. Still, stranger things had happened, and if Lilith was holding a grudge, she had succeeded in making the whole town privy to it.

"Give me a few days and I'll get back to you," he said, looping his messenger bag over his head.

"And I need to read the research Marty printed out for me and check the other stories. Call me if you have any leads."

He grinned his annoying grin. "Hey, any leads I gather on my own are mine to disclose."

She held back an eye roll. *So much for working together.*

Rob took off. As she rinsed out the coffee cups, Liz tried to imagine Lilith as the history thief. It was obvious Lilith was still angry with Sadie, but the rest of the town? It didn't fit. Still, Rob suspected Lilith was up to something. Despite her negative feelings for the reporter, he had a good nose for these things.

Which meant Lilith stayed on Liz's radar until this thing, whatever it was, was over.

———————— //////////////////////////// ————————

On Tuesday, Liz and Sarah were busy getting the fully booked inn ready for the weekend. Staying ahead of the breakfast offerings and making sure her guests were settled and had every amenity they needed during their stay, she didn't have much time for sleuthing, but the reenactment never left her mind. She'd briefly skimmed the articles she'd collected, so she had an idea of what to do. Finding active participants to portray the town founders was her next order of business.

After the breakfast crowd dwindled, Liz took a few minutes to call the community theater. She got a recording, at which she felt a flash of impatience. But her friends at Sew Welcome would know which direction to send her.

"Okay, ladies," she said as she breezed into the store, "I need to contact the person in charge of the theater. What did you say her name was?"

Mary Ann looked up from her task at the cutting table. "Amber Pierce."

"That's her." Sadie cradled the stack of quilting magazines she was placing on the display shelf. "She and her husband retired here a year ago."

"Know how I can get hold of her?"

"She works part-time at the bookstore, Once Upon a Tale," Sadie said. "When she's not working on reopening the theater."

Mary Ann smoothed the colorful fabric and readied the scissors to make her cut. "Have you come up with an idea for the reenactment?"

"I've only learned the basics, so I'm planning something simple. It'll get the job done, and I hope we can all get our belongings back."

"Oh dear," Sadie said with a laugh, "simple is far from Amber's MO."

"Meaning?"

"From what I've heard she worked off, off, off Broadway. Her motto is 'go big or go home.'"

"Let me guess. Her productions are going to be extravagant?"

"Yes. She'll want to make the signing story bigger than it is. She's angling to make a name for herself in local theater circles and with potential donors at the celebration, she'll be pushing for maximum attention. But I'm afraid there's no way around it. She does know the actors in town, so you will need to speak to her."

"I'll just have to put my foot down. No grandiose productions."

Sadie chuckled, giving Liz a "suit yourself" shrug.

"In the meantime," Mary Ann said, "we need to let the Material Girls know I've finished cutting most of the fabric for our back-to-school project. All we need is for everyone to pick up their material so we can get started on those pencil bags."

Liz walked over to the pile of cut fabric pieces. Sifting through them, she approved of Mary Ann's fabric choices. Cars and trucks; cute, fuzzy animals; and bold flower designs were a perfect selection to interest the kids who would receive the pencil bags. "I'll grab mine now," Liz said as she lifted the folded squares from the table, "and help spread the word."

"Make sure to lock up our fabric before we leave tonight," Sadie called out from across the room. Her attempt at humor rang false in the wake of the recent threats to herself and the town.

Shaking her head to clear it of negative thoughts, Liz left the store to change. The temperatures had climbed steadily each day, officially ushering in summer. After donning a sleeveless white blouse, khaki skirt, and flats, she ran a brush through her hair and set off to find Amber Pierce.

Ten minutes later, she arrived at the bookstore to find a woman shelving paperbacks near the front window.

"Amber?"

The woman turned. Her red hair was piled high, her makeup dramatic but not clownish. She looked to be about ten years older than Liz. The long, flowing handkerchief sleeves of her colorful blouse dangled from her arms as she held out a hand. Tinkling bangle bracelets circled her wrists. "And you're Liz."

Liz returned the shake with a brow drawn up quizzically.

"Sadie called ahead."

"Then you know why I'm here?"

"Yes. Let's talk."

It had been a while since Liz had explored the bookstore, but she noticed the layout had changed. A grouping of chairs now took over one corner before the front windows. The aroma of coffee hung in the air, along with the unique scent of books. It brought Liz back to her childhood days when she had frequented the Boston library and spent hours discovering new authors and wonderful adventures between the covers of a book.

"Looks like you've added shelves since the last time I was here."

"We made some upgrades since the store has started to become more popular. With more merchandise on order, new shelves were necessary."

"I saw Philip Borkholder out front the other day."

"He does fine work, but doesn't talk much." Amber placed the paperbacks on the checkout counter and faced Liz. "An older man came in to hassle Philip. Rude and angry. I had to run him off since he was upsetting the customers."

Liz felt her stomach tighten. *Thomas Sullivan.* "What was he angry about?"

"Said something about Philip accusing him of taking some old tools. Went on to say older people should be respected, not be invisible." Amber waved her hand. "It was so convoluted. I had no idea how to intervene without making matters worse."

Liz remembered the day she'd met him; Thomas hadn't been very approachable then, either.

Amber pushed back her voluminous sleeves. "Now, down to business. As you know, I'm the new director of the Pleasant Creek Playhouse."

"You must be excited."

"This is my first time in charge, so I need a flashy opening performance, you know, to make a name here. I'll be the go-to theater girl."

"I'm sure you'll succeed."

Amber beamed. "Oh, I will. Just you wait and see. I can help you round up the actors who volunteer for local productions. We're getting ready for our first show, so the timing is perfect."

"What's the next step?"

"I'll post an open casting call on the playhouse website. What day works for an audition?"

Audition? Good grief, this is becoming a bigger project than I'd imagined. "The sooner the better. We're getting down to the wire."

"How about Saturday at the theater? Noon?"

"Sounds good. I can't thank you enough for helping me."

Amber waved a heavily ringed hand. The sleeve of her blouse

tipped over a pencil jar. She began picking up the contents. "Have you settled on a script yet?"

"Um, it's not really a play. Just a reenactment."

"Doesn't mean you shouldn't have serious writers involved."

"How about I get back to you on that?"

Amber nodded, making her hair wobble. She tapped a finger on her chin. "I've been known to dabble in scriptwriting, so I can be of service."

"I'll keep that in mind." The eager gleam in the woman's eyes made Liz nervous, so she began to back out of the store. "Thanks again."

Escaping as quickly as she could, Liz made a detour to the courthouse before heading home. She was curious to see how much further along Bert had gotten with the displays. Plus, she wanted to know if he'd learned anything new about the original charter signing. She'd just stepped inside when an older woman barreled into her.

"Oof." Liz's breath left her in a puff of air. She steadied herself and glanced down in concern at the person standing before her, surprised to find it was Lilith Granger. They did a sidestep dance as each woman tried to get out of the other's way.

"Move aside," Lilith insisted. Her large leather purse was clutched to her chest.

Liz stood her ground. Here was an opportunity to speak to the woman who'd been on her mind. "I was with Sadie the other day when she stopped by your house."

The older woman blinked. "I don't remember you." Her facial expression said differently.

"Liz Eckardt."

"Nice to meet you, but now I must be going."

Before Liz could respond, Lilith rounded Liz, trying to get out the door. They collided again. Lilith's purse fell to the floor. They both bent to retrieve her bag. Lilith grabbed hold first, swiping it away from Liz's helping hand. But not before Liz glimpsed a silver bell tucked inside.

Lilith's face paled. She fled before Liz could stop her.

Just then, Bert came into the lobby with a box in hand. He stopped when he caught sight of Liz. "I wasn't expecting you."

"Hi, Bert."

"Come to check on my progress?"

"Yes, but first, was Lilith Granger here visiting you?"

His forehead wrinkled. "Heavens no. I've been alone all morning."

"Any chance you're missing a silver bell?"

"Can't say that I am. No silver bells in my inventory."

So the bell wasn't Bert's. Liz couldn't help wondering if Lilith had stolen it from someone else.

11

Back at Sew Welcome, Liz replayed her run-in with Lilith. "Do you think she's the history thief?"

A sad expression wrinkled Sadie's face. "The Lilith I knew never would have stolen from anyone. But now? I can't answer that question."

"Maybe she was bringing it to Bert to display but changed her mind," Mary Ann suggested as she went about tidying the fabric inventory.

"I thought about that," Liz said, "but why would she run off like she was guilty?"

Mary Ann placed a clip on the edge of a bolt of fabric, securing it in place. "You'd have to ask her directly to find out."

"I barely know her. She wouldn't tell me."

"And she's certainly not talking to me," Sadie interjected.

Liz blew out her cheeks. "Do you think I should call the chief?"

"And tell him what?" Mary Ann slid the bolt back into place. "That Lilith had a bell in her purse and you think she stole it?"

"Well, when you put it like that . . ."

"Who carries a bell in her purse?" Sadie wondered aloud.

"My point exactly," Liz said.

Mary Ann crossed the room. "You're both jumping to conclusions."

Sadie ignored her. "Was it big? Like a cowbell?"

"No. Small with a slim handle. I wouldn't have noticed it if her bag hadn't opened."

"Did you notice engraving or markings on it?"

"No. It happened too fast."

"Why do you ask about the engraving, Sadie?" Mary Ann asked.

"Lilith's mother had a silver tea set we played with when we were children. The bell was actually used back when the family had servants, but we just played with it and made lots of noise. It was engraved with the last letter of the family name. *G.*"

"Which makes me wonder, why doesn't she go by her husband's last name?"

"She kept her maiden name with the hopes of becoming a big movie star. Caused quite a scandal at the time."

"What was her husband's last name?"

"French. Gary French."

"Why does that name sound familiar?" Liz said.

"I suggest you two stop imagining the worst of Lilith," Mary Ann interjected. "She's probably just a lonely, bitter lady who has some quirks. Her behavior doesn't necessarily mean she's up to no good."

"I suppose." Sadie's expression softened. "Instead of suspecting her, I should try to befriend her again. When you get to be our age, it's important to look out for one another."

Liz laid a hand on Sadie's shoulder. "Do you think she'd be interested in burying the hatchet?"

"I guess there's only one way to find out. I'll have to pay her another visit."

"Which should be . . . Wait. That name—French." Liz tapped her temple. "I remember now. Rodger French was the first mayor of Pleasant Creek."

"Lilith's husband's ancestor."

"My goodness. That's a lot of names associated with the charter."

Sadie's lips formed a grim line. "Makes you wonder what Lilith really knows about the missing items."

Liz peered at Sadie. "Are you okay?"

Sadie looked away.

"You can't lie to us. We know you better than that," Mary Ann scolded.

"I haven't been sleeping well. Just last night I thought I heard someone outside the living room window. Turned out to be nothing but a case of nerves."

Mary Ann's eyes went wide. "You investigated by yourself when you know the thief has targeted you?"

"I'm not a shrinking violet."

"But you're not indestructible either," Liz added.

"Forget I mentioned it."

"After everything that's gone on around here lately," Liz said, her mind on the matters affecting them all, "I wish I could."

On Friday afternoon, Liz took a break, intending to finally read the news articles Marty had printed out for her. Settling into a chair in the sitting room, she was just about to start when the front door opened followed by a loud, "Liz. We're here."

Recognizing the voice, a big smile curved Liz's lips. She jumped up and hurried into the foyer to find Edna and Donald Hastings, a returning couple who loved the inn and, more specifically, Liz.

"You made it," Liz said in greeting.

"Indeed. Donald made good time." Edna hugged Liz. "I'm so excited to be here. And in plenty of time before the Fourth of July festivities, no less."

"Should be a real good time," Donald said after he set their suitcases down, swooping in for his hug. "Is my brother here yet?"

"Not yet. Per your request I put you in the Somewhere in Time Room and your brother and his wife will be next door in the Rose of Sharon Room."

"Excellent." Donald bobbed his head in a satisfied nod. "We haven't vacationed together in years."

"After we spoke so highly of the Olde Mansion Inn, they insisted we return and bring them along." Edna grinned. "You'll love them, Liz."

"If they're your family, I have no doubt."

"Great. Now that the pleasantries are out of the way, is there any of your wonderful cinnamon bread handy?"

"Donald!"

Liz laughed. "I'm way ahead of you. Let me give you your keys so you can get settled. Then meet me in the sitting room, and we can catch up over a few slices of cinnamon bread."

She retrieved the keys and went to grab one of the suitcases to carry upstairs when Donald stopped her. "No, my dear. I have this. You go get that bread ready."

Liz sent him a mock salute. "You got it."

While the couple settled upstairs, Liz went to the kitchen to slice the freshly baked loaf, then made sure the tall glasses were ready for iced tea before returning to the sitting room to continue her reading.

The story in the articles was consistent with what she knew. Granger, Sullivan, and Oates went to the capitol to fetch the new town charter and bring it back to Pleasant Creek. On the way home, an axle broke on the wagon. As she also knew, James Sullivan, a blacksmith, was able to fix the wagon and get them home after they fought off marauders. It all sounded like a rather dull Western movie to her.

Only one article mentioned the town celebration with the then mayor as master of ceremonies. The entire town had participated in the celebration.

"I'm right back where I started," she muttered under her breath.

She understood why the wagon wheel outside the courthouse was a landmark: It was a symbol of the humble beginnings of Pleasant

Creek. But why take it? And why the demand for a reenactment? What would inspire someone to stir up all this trouble?

She finally got to the last printout. She glanced at the banner and date. The front-page story of the *Indianapolis News* related a nearly identical account of events to the other publications, except in this article, there was no mention of an ambush. In fact, the wagon mishap was blamed on a manufacturing defect. James Sullivan was credited with fixing the problem, and they returned to Pleasant Creek with the token still in hand.

Token? What token?

She accessed the *Indianapolis News* website on her phone to locate digital copies online, and scolded herself for not thinking of it sooner. Unfortunately, the printed article already in her possession was the only mention of the Pleasant Creek charter incident.

She had to go see Bert to find out about the token.

Shoving the articles into a pile, Liz jumped up to get her purse, only to be waylaid by Edna Hastings.

"My dear, sit. Fill me in on the gossip in Pleasant Creek."

"Well, I was just—" Seeing the delight on her guest's face, she knew she couldn't run off just yet.

She sat and regaled Mrs. Hastings with the story of the history thief.

Mrs. Hastings blinked; then a slow smile turned her lips upward. "I've always told Donald that visiting Pleasant Creek is much better than seeing a movie or a play. So much excitement here."

"I can't argue with that," Liz said with a smile.

"So, you're in charge of a reenactment. Donald will be thrilled. He and his brother love anything historical."

"Then you picked a perfect time to visit."

"We did, didn't we?"

"What did we do?" Mr. Hastings asked as he entered the sitting room.

Before Liz could explain, Edna described the events that had happened recently, telling the story with much more flourish than Liz had.

"You know," Liz told them, "you should come to the auditions for the reenactment tomorrow. I'll bet I can get you a part."

Mrs. Hastings bounced in her seat. "Donald, what do you say?"

"I say we're in." He focused on Liz, but she could tell he had freshly baked bread on his mind, not reenactments.

"Cinnamon bread coming up," she said before he had a chance to remind her.

She brought a tray into the sitting room, but before Mr. Hastings could taste a piece of his beloved bread, the front door banged open. Liz hurried out to the foyer to find another couple, and judging by the man's resemblance to Donald Hastings, it had to be his brother. "Mr. and Mrs. Hastings?"

"Call me Ronald," he boomed. "And this is my wife, Tippy."

The other couple came from the sitting room to greet their family with hugs and kisses.

"I've put you in the Rose of Sharon Room." Liz gave the new couple the keys to their room. "How about we head upstairs?"

She gave the quick tour for first-time guests before encouraging them to get settled and then come down for refreshments. When she returned to the sitting room, Edna had moved the stack of articles in front of her and was engrossed in one of them. Donald was nowhere in sight, and Liz imagined he had absconded with a slice or two of cinnamon bread to the four-season room, one of his favorite haunts in the inn.

"Liz, dear, where is the Sullivan Ironworks?"

Liz sat next to her. "Pardon?"

Edna folded the paper. "See here, off to the side? It says Sullivan

Ironworks provided not only the materials to fix the wagon, but also provided funding for the signing celebration. It looks like an advertisement."

"What?" Liz took the page Edna handed her. She scanned the article, realizing that in her rush to get the details she'd missed this fact. She'd been concentrating on the articles, not the ads.

She lowered the paper to her lap. "So if Sullivan Ironworks was a big part of the charter signing, was the Sullivan family more involved than the Granger, Oates, and French families?"

"If they were, what would that mean, Liz?"

"I don't know for sure, probably nothing. But I'm back to the bottom line. The reenactment must be presented in order for things to get back to normal around here."

"With you at the helm, this history thief is in for a rude awakening," Edna huffed.

Soon, Ronald and Tippy joined them and Donald returned, a few stray crumbs still dotting the front of his shirt. The talk turned to family. Feeling like a fifth wheel, Liz replenished the iced-tea pitcher and made sure there was enough bread to go around.

After another trip to the kitchen, Liz heard a rapid knocking coming from the utility room. Nearly tripping over Beans, who decided to break protocol and accompany Liz to the door, she opened it to find the doorstep empty. Or so it appeared.

Beans waddled outside and sat beside an envelope lying on the cement. With a loud woof, he made his presence known to whomever had dropped it off. Liz bent down and gave the dog's head a rub. Then she retrieved the mystery envelope, unable to ignore the creepy sense of being watched. She scanned the area around the inn, but nothing appeared out of the ordinary.

"C'mon, boy," she urged and hustled them both inside. In the kitchen, she poured kibble into Beans's bowl. As the bulldog happily munched away, Liz opened the flap of the envelope to remove a letter written in red ink with a heavy hand.

Time is counting down. The reenactment had better be correct, or there will be more fireworks on the Fourth of July than Pleasant Creek is counting on.

The history thief apparently knew she was in charge and had decided to make her the next target of his threats.

Liz was aware of the time constraints, but still couldn't figure out what the thief really wanted. Recognition? To right a wrong? To cause havoc? Without knowing the motivation, a harmless misrepresentation might be perceived as wrong.

She found her cell phone and took a picture of the note. She'd get the original document to the chief, but first, she had to call Rob Carver. She'd give him a new story to run with—one that might help Liz in the long run.

The history thief had made a mistake by bringing the fight to Liz's doorstep.

12

"Let's start by looking at this from Lilith's point of view," Liz said later that night.

Gathered in the sitting room after Sew Welcome had closed for business and her guests had retired upstairs, Liz, Sadie, and Mary Ann, who'd asked Jackson over for the discussion, agreed that Lilith and Thomas both had reasons to be upset. But were those reasons enough to justify theft and threats? Liz took notes while they talked and referred to the ones she'd already made.

"Lilith's forefather was one of the men to bring the charter to town. She was also married to a descendant of Rodger French, the mayor at the time of the signing," Liz read from her notebook. "Based on her behavior, we suspect she's up to something, but don't know what."

"She sure looks guilty," Sadie said.

"But is innocent until proven otherwise," Mary Ann reminded her. "And the chief hasn't uncovered any evidence of wrongdoing; otherwise, he would have arrested her by now."

Jackson shook his head. "With the absence of any new clues, the investigation is at a standstill."

"So we keep forging ahead," Liz said. "Next, we have Thomas Sullivan. His family also has deep roots in Pleasant Creek. Jackson, you mentioned something about an iron marker being stolen from the wagon during the ambush?"

"That's the town lore."

"So does Sullivan Ironworks somehow fit into this story?" Liz said.

"Why do you ask?"

"I found an article from the time period mentioning the factory. It looks like they underwrote the first celebration."

"Why? Just for goodwill or did they want something in return?" Jackson rubbed a hand over his jaw, apparently preoccupied.

"My thoughts exactly," Liz replied. "There was also mention of a token. Could the article be referring to the iron marker?"

"Without more information, we can't know why this fact would be important." Jackson rested his elbows on his knees and leaned into the conversation. "There was never any marker from the ironworks attached to a building in town, as far as I know."

Liz tapped her pen on the notebook. "At least it's more information than we started out with."

Sadie perked up. "So we go back to visit Thomas and get more details about the token. Or we visit Lilith again and find out what she's up to."

"We?" Mary Ann asked, brows raised.

"I'm not going to sit at home like a bump on a log."

"Like we could force you to do that, Sadie," Jackson said, his tone affectionate.

"So what do you intend to do?" Sadie countered.

"Liz and I will interview Lilith. We have no history with her. She might let her guard down with us."

"And Thomas likes to talk about the ironworks," Liz said. "We can get his take on the token."

Mary Ann nodded. "I agree. Sadie, as badly as I'm sure you want to be involved, you need to keep your head down until this is all over. If ever there was a time to be sensible, this is it."

Jackson turned to Liz. "Busy tomorrow?"

"I'm meeting with some of the playhouse actors to audition for the reenactment, but that's not until noon."

"What do you say we visit Lilith and Thomas beforehand?"

"Sounds like a plan." Liz paused. "What do you think about Amber?" she asked the group.

Sadie perked up. "Amber? What about her?"

"When I spoke to her at the bookstore, there was this intensity about her. Reopening the playhouse is important to her. And she loves a splash. What if she has something to do with the missing items? What better way to create a story and spotlight the playhouse in the process?"

"How would she know about the history?" Mary Ann countered.

"With Heritage Day coming up, she's bound to have heard about the reason for the celebration."

"But why risk getting caught?" Jackson said. "That isn't good publicity."

"Maybe she thinks she'll be in the limelight when the items are returned," Liz continued, on a roll. "If they show up anonymously, she's got a great premise for her next play."

Jackson shook his head. "If you go with that reasoning, the same could be said about Bert. He needs historical pieces for his display or his dreams go up in smoke."

"And that doesn't explain the threats," Mary Ann added.

"I didn't see any of the missing items when I was in Bert's office." Liz frowned. "And Amber might simply be ambitious. I guess that blows my theory."

"The chief has the inventory of Bert's collection. If Stan has any suspicions, he knows where to look." Jackson stood. "Ladies, I'm going to head home. Anyone need a ride?"

"No, we both brought our own cars." Mary Ann rose and collected her purse. "I'll be here bright and early to open the shop, so it's time for me to call it a night. Sadie?"

Sadie remained in her chair, a thoughtful expression on her face. "You go on. I'll be leaving soon."

Mary Ann shot Liz a concerned look, but strode off with Jackson. Liz remained on the couch and waited. Sadie clearly had something on her mind.

"What if this is my fault?" she asked, her voice desolate.

"Yours? Sadie, why would you think such a thing?"

"Lilith is angry with me. I'm a member of the historical society, which was responsible for leaving Lilith out of the Heritage Day plans. Put the two together and I have one woman I've offended twice over."

"First of all, you haven't really spoken to Lilith in ages, right? And secondly, you don't run the society. The undelivered letters were an oversight by Wanda and Rosemarie. It's nothing you could have planned for or controlled."

"But this feels personal."

Liz leaned over and patted Sadie's hand. "Yes. And it feels that way to every single person who had something stolen from them."

"I think seeing Lilith again has brought up a lot of buried emotions. Some conflicted, some good." She paused. "Lilith and I were friends, Liz. How could I ever have let us get to this place?"

Liz saw that Sadie was finally revealing the root of her anguish: She felt guilt about a friendship lost, not about stolen material things. Her estrangement from Lilith held more sentimental value than a pile of antiques ever could.

"Life isn't always smooth. Things happen. We move on. I don't know if there's any one answer to your question. Besides, Lilith had a say in the outcome too."

"I suppose." Sadie smoothed her skirt. "I always said I didn't want to look back at my life with regrets. I've made decisions and lived with them. Losing Lilith's friendship is one aspect I'll always wish I'd handled differently."

"If you don't want regrets, do something about it."

She gave Liz a sad smile. "It seems too late."

"You're the one who is always encouraging us to live out our dreams. To go after the things we want. If making amends with Lilith is important, then do it."

Sadie's smile warmed a little. "Lately it feels as though people keep throwing my words back at me."

"That's because they're wise words. Spoken to us by a caring woman."

"Some days I would argue that."

"Just think about it. As long as you and Lilith are still on this earth, there's a chance to make things right."

"I'll give the situation some thought." With a sigh, Sadie rose. "I should get home."

"Are you sure you don't want to stay with somebody? I don't know about you, but I've been skittish lately."

A stubborn scowl came over Sadie's face. "Liz Eckardt, I can take care of myself."

"No one says you can't. But too much pride comes before a fall."

"Are you trying to make a point?"

"Just trying out some wise words of my own. Is it working?"

Sadie chuckled. "I will think about what you said."

"That's all I can ask."

———

The next morning, after feeding the Hastingses and the other Olde Mansion Inn guests, Liz changed into a green patterned blouse, skirt, and flats before Jackson arrived. She had jotted down a list of questions last night and hoped the day's visits would go smoother than the last time.

While she waited for Jackson, she printed the outline she'd drafted the night before to give to the actors at the audition. She'd listed the cast of characters: the mayor and the three heroes of the story. She'd also written dialogue and added stage directions to the best of her ability. She hoped she had enough written that Amber and the seasoned actors could take hold of her words and spice them up with dramatic flair. With so much at stake, she didn't want to bomb at her first-time directorial debut.

Right at ten, Jackson walked into the inn, dressed casually in a dark T-shirt and jeans. "Ready?"

She tidied the stack of papers on her desk. "You bet. Let me get my purse."

When she returned from her quarters, Jackson had begun pacing in the foyer, his phone to his ear.

"You're sure about this?" He paused. "I'll be right there." Jackson ended the call.

"What's going on?" Liz asked.

"We have a situation."

Her stomach churned. "Four words I never like to hear."

He led her to the sitting room. When they were seated, he said, "Bert had something stolen from his collection."

"When I asked him if any of his antiques had gone missing, he said no."

"He wasn't entirely forthcoming."

By the look on his face, she knew this was bad. "Do I want to know?"

"Remember the knife you found embedded in your tire?"

She pictured it clearly. "Not likely I'll forget."

"The knife is Bert's missing piece. The chief matched it to the description on Bert's list."

Liz's heart thudded in her chest. "Could Bert be the history thief?"

Jackson shrugged, his face grim. "I wouldn't have thought so.

Chief Houghton says Bert claims he had no idea it was missing until the chief brought it to his attention. I'm heading to the department now, so I'm afraid today's outing will have to be rescheduled."

"I understand. Go see what the chief has to say."

He tilted his head. Liz could read the hesitation there.

"Are you sure? You look a little shaky," Jackson said.

"I am, but I'll pull it together." *Bert?* She didn't want to believe he had anything to hide, but he couldn't explain away the knife. "Besides, I've got that appointment at the playhouse so I should get my head in the game."

"I'm sorry I roped you into volunteering to stage the reenactment. I'd understand if you want to back out."

"Jackson, despite everything that's been going on, I still want to do this."

"You're sure? Because I can find someone else."

"No. There's not enough time now anyway. I can handle it."

He smiled. "I know you can."

"Thanks for the vote of confidence." She thought about having to work with actors, a totally new endeavor for her, and said, "I hope this works."

Jackson stood. "I'll let you know what I find out."

"Be careful."

He sent her a gentle smile. "Always." He left.

Poor Bert. He'd seemed sure his antiques had gone untouched, yet the knife that had cut into her tire was from his collection. She might not know him very well, but it was no secret how important the display was to him. Was it important enough to steal for? Did it mean so much to him that he would threaten his fellow townspeople just to get his way?

As a group of women exited Sew Welcome, Liz tucked away her

thoughts and glanced at her watch. Another Saturday morning class had ended. With time to kill before heading to the playhouse, Liz made her way into the shop.

"Good morning, ladies," she called out.

"Is it?" Sadie grouched. "I'm glad that class is over with."

Mary Ann came up beside Liz. "Nerves are on edge this morning. The town thefts are making everyone a little short-tempered."

"And it keeps getting worse." Liz explained about the knife.

Mary Ann looked surprised. "Bert?"

"I'm afraid so."

"We only have a week before Heritage Day," Mary Ann said. "With the expected turnout for the celebration, how on earth will the chief keep everyone safe?"

"I'm sure the burden is not lost on him." Liz lifted her shoulders. "But the thief has to make a mistake sometime, right? This can't go on."

"And what if word gets out about what's been happening in Pleasant Creek? The business owners have already spent a great deal of money on the big day. If tourist spending is down, we're sunk."

"Let's hope it doesn't come to that. If I get enough of the reenactment right, we'll get our belongings back. That is, if the thief intends to keep his promise."

"I'm beginning to wonder . . ." Mary Ann began.

"Don't you turn negative on me now."

"Sorry. I guess I'm still worried about Sadie. She feels guilty about Lilith. Plus, she told me she didn't sleep well last night. Every sound she heard during the night made her jump."

"I asked if she wanted to stay with someone last night."

"And you knew she'd turn you down."

They glanced across the room to see Sadie struggling to push a bolt of fabric back between the others on the shelf, muttering while she put her weight into it.

"She needs a break." Liz walked over to her friend. "Sadie, I need your help."

Sadie glanced up at Liz. "I know that look. I'm okay, and I'm not leaving the shop."

"If you insist. I'm going to the playhouse to find actors for the reenactment. I just thought you might be able to pick out the folks best suited for the roles. And I'm sure we'll need a costuming consultation."

"Are you trying to bribe me into tagging along?"

"Is it working?"

Sadie grinned. "Let me get my hat."

As Sadie went to the counter, Liz walked back to Mary Ann. "I'm taking Sadie with me to the reenactment auditions."

"Thanks. Giving her something to focus on will get her mind off things. The stress is getting to her, even if she won't admit it."

"Going to the playhouse won't get her mind off Lilith since they worked together there, but helping me direct? That should do the trick."

Mary Ann laughed. "True. She loves to take charge." A customer walked through the door. Catching a glimpse of Mary Ann, the woman started in their direction.

"Back to work. Keep Sadie out of trouble."

"Is that even possible?"

Liz turned to find Sadie at her side, a bright-yellow, wide-brimmed hat perched on her head. "Let's get a move on."

"You got it."

Fifteen minutes later, Liz parked in front of the theater. The marquee showcased the words "Pleasant Creek Playhouse." The entire sign, outlined in red when turned on, consisted of lights seeming to chase each other around the square box. Big, bold letters announced

"Soon to be Reopened." A flat overhang covered the entrance to the building as well as the box office, a small glassed-in area to the right of the main entrance.

They made their way through the double front doors of the playhouse. Liz paused a moment, taking in her surroundings. She'd been to a few Broadway plays and had always loved visiting theaters in Manhattan, but the Pleasant Creek Playhouse took her by surprise.

The lavish lobby was covered in crimson carpet, which extended to the stairs leading to the second level. Gold damask curtains pulled back with thick, braided ties outlined the theater doors on either side of the concession stand. Indistinguishable voices floated through the arched openings.

"Must be this way," Liz said, following the direction of the voices. They passed under the curtains and stopped at the back of the seating area, the aisle on a decline leading to the stage. The lighting was dim, so Liz walked alongside Sadie, ready to lend a steadying hand if necessary. Not that Sadie would accept it.

The stage curtains were open and a spotlight shone overhead, illuminating the area on the floor before the stage. About fifteen people sat in the first and second center rows, Edna and Donald Hastings among them. Amber Pierce spoke with sweeping hand gestures, her bangle bracelets a musical symphony accompanying her lyrical words.

"And here she is now." Amber turned in Liz's direction. "The woman responsible for our next production."

"Reenactment," Liz corrected. "It's nothing more than a simple revisiting of history."

"Yes, of course," Amber agreed, her brow furrowed. She seemed to float as she walked, landing next to Liz. "Although in light of the events going on in town, I think we have an original on our hands. I've already started penning a story concept I want to turn into a script."

"We should focus on the charter signing first."

"Yes." She waved her hand in a theatrical arch again. "Please, begin."

Liz took the copies of her outlines from her bag before facing the crowd. She recognized a few people, merchants from local shops mostly. To her surprise, Claire Sullivan sat amongst the group. She didn't know why it surprised her, but after she thought about it, Claire being here would be great if Liz needed perspective from a Sullivan point of view.

"Thanks so much for coming," said Liz. "As you have probably heard, the mayor would like us to perform a short reenactment of the town charter signing on Heritage Day." She handed the stack of papers to the person on the end of each row to pass along. "I have outlined the main characters. For that, I will need four men. The rest of you can fill in as townspeople excited to be a part of history. There is limited dialogue, attributed mostly to the actor portraying the first mayor."

A hand raised. "Are there any action scenes, like the ambush on the wagon trip home from the State House?"

"Not in this version. We'll be focusing on the charter signing alone."

Another person spoke out. "How about the use of firearms? I know how to use fake gunpowder safely."

"Um . . . we're just going to use fountain pens."

"Are there any death scenes?"

Good grief! "I don't recall reading about anyone dying during the charter signing."

Disappointed mutters reverberated through the group. Amber spoke up. "Pity. There is nothing more challenging for an actor than a death scene."

"For our purposes, we are sticking with the facts as I have researched them."

Edna Hastings raised her hand. "You know, Liz, using this reenactment might be a good way to smoke out the real thief. If we rewrite history, this person will most likely want to show up to correct us and, bam, he's caught."

"Or he'll sabotage Heritage Day if we get it wrong," said an elderly man seated in the middle of the first row. "That's when the drama would really begin."

As if the drama isn't already ongoing? Liz bit her lip, fighting the mounting pressure of getting this reenactment right. If anyone in this town got hurt, the blame would fall at her feet.

13

"No changing history. No death scenes. No firearms," Liz listed. What had she gotten herself into?

"If you insist," Amber sniffed.

Sadie sidled up to Liz. "Best move ahead before this crowd gets any more bloodthirsty."

Liz couldn't have agreed more.

"Okay. Let the men gather to the right side of the stage. We'll run through some lines to see who fits the parts," Liz said.

As the men rose, the ladies moved in closer together to chat and gossip. Sadie joined them, leaving Liz and Amber to select the actors for the parts.

"Liz, no offense, but there's no conflict in this story."

"Amber, I think there's enough real-life conflict going on to keep the players happy."

"From a theatrical point of view, we want to wow the audience."

"The only person we need to wow is the thief. Once he gets what he wants, hopefully this whole farce will be over."

Amber shrugged. "Whatever. Carry on."

Liz faced the men. There were various ages represented. According to her research, the mayor had been older while the three men in the wagon were most likely in their early thirties.

She singled out a man who looked to be in his fifties, with graying hair and a mustache. "Your name?"

"Kendell Parker, at your service," he drawled in a Southern accent, followed by a courtly bow.

"Would you please read the mayor's lines for me?"

The man shook his paper, then cleared his throat. "On behalf of Pleasant Creek," his deep voice boomed, "I welcome you to the first Heritage Day celebration. We have much to be proud of, and we have these three men to thank," he paused to wave his arm to his left, "for making the day possible." He finished and looked at Liz. "I can do it again more convincingly. I just need a bit more time to get into character."

"No need. It was great," Liz called out.

Amber hustled over and whispered. "You should have him recite his lines again. We never pick parts with only one read-through."

"Good to know," Liz whispered back. "Please, Kendell, could you read the lines again?"

Kendell repeated the words, this time portraying the mayor as more puffed up. The lines were exaggerated, but still good. Liz called on three other men to read the mayor's lines to get a good sampling before making a decision.

"Thanks to all of you. Now I need to find my Sullivan, Granger, and Oates."

Liz had the younger men line up. They got into their interpretation of character and even though they only had a few lines each, Liz soon had a good idea of whom to cast as the Pleasant Creek founders.

To her surprise, time flew by as the actors took on their roles. She didn't know what she'd expected, but the level of professionalism pleased her. She hoped the thief would appreciate the portrayals, which were as accurate as she could make them with the information she had. "Let's take a break," she said after an hour had passed.

The actors milled around, discussing the ways they could bring the parts to life.

"You have a knack," Sadie told her as she appeared by Liz's side.

"I don't know. I think I was less nervous before my bar exam." Liz glanced at the actors, who were chatting with each other. Amber was nowhere to be seen. "Does Amber seem a little intense to you?"

"Passion could be mistaken for intensity."

"No, it's more. She seems very invested in this 'production.'"

"Liz, it may be nothing."

"Or it may be everything."

"You don't want to believe Bert could be guilty so you're grasping at straws," Sadie accused.

"True, I don't want to think the worst of Bert, but there's something up with Amber."

Sadie patted Liz's back and said, "Try to have fun," before walking away to join the actors.

As Sadie walked away, Liz turned to grab a pen from her tote bag. A movement in the back of the theater caught her eye, but the theater was too dark and the shadow was moving too fast for her to distinguish what she saw. She waited to see if anything moved again, but nothing happened.

"So," Edna said as she joined Liz. "Any thoughts on who might play the mayor's wife?"

Liz knew where this was going but played along. "Let me guess. You want the part?"

Edna clasped her hands in front of her chest and nodded. "This is so much fun."

Liz glanced around the room. "I suppose it's only fair I take a look at the actresses who came out today."

"And then you'll pick me?"

Liz laughed. "We'll see."

The break ended and Liz rounded up the women. A few had used the break to visit the restroom and returned in a pack, Amber included. Although there were no speaking parts, she did have to match up the women who looked like they could be the wives of her leading men. She wasn't sure what to do with Claire, since she was a Sullivan, but decided to keep her as a town resident. After talking to the women, she had her cast picked out.

Asking the actors to take a seat, Liz stood before them again. "Thanks so much for coming out today. I know it's last minute, but I think we'll pull off this reenactment successfully. When I call out your name, I'll announce your part and we'll start our first rehearsal."

Amber stood and scurried over to her side. "Usually we go a few days before announcing parts. You know, to ramp up excitement."

"Amber, the reenactment is scheduled in a week. We have to start today."

The bracelets at Amber's wrists rattled as she flapped her hands with annoyance. "Fine. Have it your way."

Liz closed her eyes and breathed deeply before facing the crowd again. "Here we go."

She read off the names she'd listed on her master outline. Kendell for the part of mayor, and three of the younger men for the heroes. Then she announced the wives, choosing Edna as the mayor's wife. Her squeal pierced Liz's ears and reduced everyone to laughter.

"For those who didn't get a specific part, we need you to be townspeople. Just improvise. Those of you with speaking parts, take a few minutes to run through your lines and then we'll get started."

This statement brought a narrow-eyed glare from Amber, but the remaining actors agreed to do their parts. Even with their cooperation, Liz knew that her first time in the theater would likely be her last.

The group positioned themselves to act out the scene. A few

women, including Edna and another woman with her back to Liz, hovered in the wings. Others spread out over the stage. Liz seized on an idea to make the rehearsal run more smoothly. "Amber, could I speak with you a moment?"

The woman made her way to Liz, the sound of her bangles and beaded necklace heralding her approach.

"I'd like to take a look at the costume selection. Would you mind prepping the group for a rehearsal?"

Amber perked up. "Yes, of course." She dug into the pocket of her jeans and pulled out a key ring. She selected one and handed it to Liz. "This will open the costume and prop room."

Liz handed her the master outline in exchange for the keys. "If you think of anything I left out, please let me know." With her limited experience and the time crunch, Liz was bound to have omitted something.

Amber smiled and, in her element, clapped her hands to draw the attention of the actors.

Pointing to Sadie, Liz motioned her friend over. "How about checking out the costumes with me? I could use some expert advice."

"My pleasure."

They set off backstage to the hallway and rooms beyond.

"Are you doing okay?" Liz asked. "I wanted your help today, not to force you to walk down memory lane."

"Being here brings back lots of memories. More good than bad. In the years following the falling out with Lilith, I still volunteered to work on the costumes. Of course, since the playhouse has been closed, I haven't been back." She smiled. "Don't worry Liz, I'm fine."

"Just say the word if you want to leave."

"You know I will."

They headed down the long hallway.

"Here, on the right," Sadie instructed.

Liz unlocked the door. She flipped the switch to find a neatly organized room with rows of movable wardrobe racks overstuffed with clothing. Shelves of hats and other accessories like leather belts and colorful scarves took over one wall. Just underneath stretched a long shoe rack.

"This place is very well stocked."

Sadie smiled. "Remember, the playhouse was open for many years."

As Liz neared a rack, she noticed a faint musty smell. "Some of these outfits must be old."

"We never threw away anything if we could help it. 'Repurpose' was our motto." Sadie ran her fingers over the outfits nearest her. "Only if the material had become threadbare did we throw it away. Otherwise, that's where I came in. With my trusty sewing machine, I could fix any costume malfunction they threw my way."

"Did you create any of your own designs?"

"From time to time. If a director had a specific vision, I could make a suitable costume."

"I bet the actresses loved you."

"Oh, they did." She chuckled. "I remember one time Lilith had a role—I can't recall what it was now—but she wore a beautiful flowing gown. She was a vision. Just before the curtain rose on opening night, the heel of her shoe tangled in the hem and ripped the material. She was so upset. I thought she would burst into tears, which would have made things doubly bad because she was already nervous."

"What did you do?"

"I dashed over with my needle and thread, and quickly stitched up the tear." Sadie's smile disappeared. "It was one of the last nice moments we shared together."

Liz placed her hands on her hips and scanned the space. "Where do you suggest we begin?"

"I'll start on one side. You take the other."

Liz was passing the open door to start her search when she heard a heavy bumping in the hallway. She paused and then looked over her shoulder to make sure Sadie was occupied before poking her head out the door. The hallway was quiet and empty in both directions. Could the noise have come from the actors working on the reenactment scene on stage? It made sense, since they weren't too far away.

"Liz, the costumes?" Sadie called out.

"Right." She made her way to the nearest rack and started going through the inventory. "Most of the dresses are too modern for our needs."

"Here we go." Sadie's voice floated from deep in the racks on the other side of the room. Liz made her way over to find Sadie holding up a hanger with a long, pioneer-style dress. "What do you think?"

"Looks like the right time period to me. I looked up clothing designs on the Internet last night to get an idea of what we needed. These will work."

"There are enough dresses for the women, but we're going to need to repair them." Sadie stuck her finger through the torn stitching. "Some of the seams are split, and the hems are raveling."

"What about the men's costumes?"

"Same. They're good enough for a short play, but they'll also need to be mended."

"At least we have a large selection to choose from."

Sadie handed Liz the hanger with the dress. "Let me pull out the costumes we need. Then we can match sizes with the actors."

For the next few minutes, they worked to choose different-size clothing. Liz hung their selections on an empty rack she found behind the open door.

"How long will it take to do the mending?" she asked.

"Not long." Sadie's eyes brightened. "I'll get the teen sewing class to work with us. What better way to teach them about civic duty than to get them to work together to support the town?"

"And keep them off their cell phones?"

"That too."

Liz had just hung another assortment of clothing on the rack when a loud bump sounded, as if someone had fallen against the wall, followed by a clatter. She rushed out of the room, just catching a glimpse of someone leaving through a side door at the end of the hallway.

Sadie came up behind her.

"Where does that door go?" Liz asked.

"To the alley between the theater and the building next door."

"Stay here."

Liz took off after the person, pushing open the door. The bright sunlight stopped her short, causing her to squint. Shading her eyes with her hands, she jogged down the few steps and hurried through the empty alley to the sidewalk, nearly colliding with a few people walking by. The bags they carried indicated they were shoppers, not the mysterious figure who'd been lurking inside the theater.

"I know I heard and saw something," she said under her breath. She stood there a few moments, but no one suspicious caught her eye. Taking a few steps down the sidewalk, she peered into the window of the drugstore. To her surprise, Lilith Granger stood in an aisle, placing merchandise in a store basket.

Liz slipped inside the store, blocking Lilith's path.

"Wh-what are you doing?" Lilith asked, her chest heaving, as if she had exerted too much energy.

Chasing you through an alley, perhaps? "I'd like to ask you some questions."

Lilith's face lost color. Her eyes darted to and fro as she looked around the room for an escape.

"Who are you to ask me questions?" Lilith finally said. She hugged her purse to her chest, dropping her shopping basket. She tried to dodge Liz, but Liz stopped her.

Liz went into lawyer mode. "I know you were spying."

Lilith stepped back and stared at Liz. "Spying on what?"

"The reenactment rehearsal at the theater."

"I've been shopping, not spying," Lilith said with a little more spirit this time.

"Really? You just happen to be in a store next to the theater right after I heard someone knocking around the hallway?"

"I can assure you, I was not in the theater." Her eyes narrowed. "I haven't stepped foot in that place in years."

The conviction in the older woman's voice gave Liz pause. Liz almost believed her.

"Is there a problem?" the clerk asked as she crossed the sales floor.

"Has Mrs. Granger been in the store for very long?"

The clerk looked at Lilith, who swayed back and forth, hugging her bag closer to her body. "Well, I didn't notice her coming in, but she is pretty much a regular every Saturday afternoon at this time."

Lilith nodded. "I have a set routine each week." She gestured to her dropped shopping basket, which contained toiletries. "I've been here for at least fifteen minutes."

Liz suddenly felt foolish. Here she was, harassing an old lady in the middle of her weekly shopping. But there was something off, and Liz couldn't discount her gut feeling. Lilith was hiding something.

"What about the other day, when I saw you at the courthouse? You were acting oddly then too."

Lilith squared her shoulders. "What I was doing is none of your concern. When you've lived in this town as long as I have, then you can question my actions. Until then, leave me alone."

Lilith swept out of the store, leaving her basket on the floor.

"She's not that bad," the clerk said. "Just lonely, I think."

Was loneliness a good enough reason for someone to steal and make threats? As much as Liz wanted to follow her, she probably wouldn't learn anything. Lilith was on high alert.

Retracing her steps to the side door of the theater, Liz found Sadie hovering in the doorway. "Well?" Sadie said.

"I had a run-in with Lilith."

"Do you think she was in here?"

"I can't be sure." Liz stepped back inside the hallway and yanked the door shut, draping them in shadows. "*If* anyone was here at all. It might have been my imagination. The noise we heard may have been anything."

"Oh, someone was here." Sadie gestured to a broom handle laying on the floor outside the slightly ajar utility closet door.

Liz opened the door wider. Inside, a few jugs of cleaning solution had been tipped over. Had someone been hiding out here? Why?

"I thought I saw a moving shadow earlier during the auditions, but figured it was just my eyes playing tricks in the dim lighting. But after this . . ." Liz shook her head. "I have to think someone was spying on us."

"It would seem that way."

Liz shivered.

"If it is our thief," Sadie reasoned, "at least he's seen we're taking the threats seriously by working on the reenactment."

"Or he—or she—has seen that I've made a mess of it."

"Either way, we know someone is watching."

14

Liz held another rehearsal at the theater Monday night. Amber helped her with blocking the scene, which Liz learned meant deciding where the actors would stand at various points in the reenactment. Although still spooked at the thought of someone watching their earlier practice, Liz was determined to carry on as though nothing had happened.

She'd thought about calling Chief Houghton after the audition, but just as quickly decided against it. Other than the open closet door and her bad feeling, there was no proof anyone had been hiding in the theater.

"Okay, Kendell," she said as the cast stood in position, "you are speaking to the town at large. Go."

"Dear town citizens. On behalf of Pleasant Creek . . ."

The actor repeated his lines, memorized now. As he strode back and forth in front of the other actors, he waved a hand to his side, knocking into one of the townsfolk. She cried out and stepped back, her heel pressing down on the top of another man's foot. He jumped, losing his balance. As he teetered, he grabbed the shoulder of the person beside him and they both went down. The cast moved from their places, speaking over each other as they circled the men on the floor.

Mary Ann, who had tagged along with Sadie after work in order to help with the costume sizing, watched with a horrified look on her face. Sadie threw up her hands and waded into the melee. It was several minutes before the confusion abated and everyone calmed down.

"Are you okay?" Liz asked one of the men.

"My foot's gonna hurt tomorrow." He glared at the woman who'd stepped on him. She scowled back.

"Blame it on Kendell. He smacked me."

"Not on purpose, I assure you."

Irritated voices rose again.

"People!" Liz called out. "Please. Take five."

Some of the cast wandered over to the table where Liz had placed bottles of water. Others huddled in small groups.

"This is a disaster." She covered her face with her hands.

Mary Ann threw an arm over Liz's shoulders. "No one said it would be easy."

Liz dropped her hands and sent a sidelong look at her friend. "Herding cats would be easier at this point."

"Not Siamese," Sadie said as she passed by. "They won't listen to anyone."

"Is it me?" Liz asked. "Or is everyone in Pleasant Creek on edge?"

"They are. Until the thief's identity is uncovered, I expect tensions to keep rising," Mary Ann said.

"Oh, Liz," Edna Hastings asked as she joined the women, "are we calling it a night?"

"No. We have too much work to do."

"Speaking of," Sadie said, "Mary Ann and I will roll the racks on stage so we can hand out the costumes."

"Great. I'll run through the scene again."

"Excuse me." Claire Sullivan held up a hand. "I know we practiced the other day, but I was wondering if I might make a suggestion for the Sullivan actor? My husband gave me a few insights I think might be important."

Liz walked her way. "What kind of information?"

"The wagon wheel was present at the signing, according to family history. We should place it . . . well, I mean a replica since the original's been stolen, in the scene."

Liz considered. "That would add more authenticity."

"Thomas says he can fashion a new wheel in time for the reenactment."

"Tell him to go ahead."

Claire beamed before returning to her position in the scene.

Getting the cast back together, Liz asked them to start from the top. This time the group spread farther apart instead of the tight arrangement Amber had rehearsed previously, but Liz didn't correct the issue. She didn't want any more calamities. They'd just gotten underway when Mary Ann appeared at her side.

"I need to speak to you."

"Now?"

Mary Ann nodded furiously.

"Take five," Liz called to the group on stage.

Murmurs came from the actors as Mary Ann pulled Liz far from earshot.

"What happened now?"

"The costumes you and Sadie picked out the other day are missing."

"Missing? Are you sure?"

"The whole rack is gone."

Liz stared at her friend. "This is crazy. Where could the costumes be?"

Shock gave way to anger as Liz stomped backstage. "This person sure isn't making it easy to deliver on the demands."

They arrived at the costume room to find Sadie busy picking through the racks. "Not much in way of replacement outfits."

"What are we going to do?"

"Well, we're not going to panic," came Sadie's calm reply. "We'll figure this out."

"Can you sew enough costumes in time for the reenactment?" Liz asked, knowing it was impossible.

Mary Ann shook her head. "Liz, you're talking about five days."

"Liz. Oh, Liz," a singsong voice came from outside the room.

"I need to get back out there. See what you two can come up with before we set off a frenzy."

Liz hurried into the hallway to find Edna Hastings heading her way. "There you are. We were getting worried when you just ran off."

"I . . . um . . . had to answer a costume question." She strode toward Edna and turned her in the direction of the stage. "Let's get back to work."

"Liz, the cast was talking, and we wonder if perhaps there should be more speaking lines."

"No," Liz rushed to say. She was already in over her head. "I mean, let's keep it simple for right now. But thanks for bringing it to my attention."

"Are you okay? Your eye is twitching."

Mumbling something about too little sleep and too much caffeine, she dismissed Edna's observation and shuffled Edna back with the others. They'd just launched back into the scene when a squeaky rattle from the back of the theater grew closer. Liz turned toward the racket and shielded her eyes from the spotlight. A long, rolling costume rack came into view. She stepped to the edge of the stage to find Amber pushing the rack.

"Hello, Liz. Hello, everyone," she said in her upbeat voice.

"What's this?" Liz asked.

Amber looked at the clothing, then back to Liz. "The costumes, of course."

"*You* took them?"

"I needed to take inventory for when the cast claims their outfits.

The clothing also needed to be laundered since we haven't used these particular costumes in ages." She blinked when she realized Liz was staring at her. "Is there a problem?"

"A big problem. We thought they'd been stolen."

"Stolen?" Amber repeated, confused.

"Stolen?" Claire blurted loudly behind Liz, bringing about another round of jumbled conversation.

Liz felt the first throb of a headache. Holding up her hand, she shushed the cast.

"I'm so sorry," Amber rushed to say. "I was trying to help."

Was she? Amber wanted to be in charge of this production and Liz stood in her way. "It was a misunderstanding," Liz replied, her blood pressure slowly returning to normal. If it hadn't been for the idea that someone had been watching them the other day, she wouldn't have been so upset. "It was thoughtful of you."

Sadie and Mary Ann arrived back on stage.

"Oh. The costumes are back," Sadie said in a calm tone, as plainly as if she were commenting on the weather.

Liz looked at Sadie, who shrugged. "I guess I never thought about Amber taking them."

"It's water under the bridge. Why don't we take a break from acting and focus on the clothing for now?" Liz said.

As Amber, Sadie, and Mary Ann took over sizing the actors, Liz took advantage of the free time to catch her breath. She went to the lobby and out the front door, eager for fresh air. Insects buzzed in the balmy evening. The sun was setting, painting the sky a golden hue. A single car motored by, leaving Liz to enjoy the silence alone. After the chaos of the run-through, the quiet washed over her, allowing her a measure of peace.

Down the street, a group of people filed out of town hall, Jackson bringing up the rear. Most went to their cars or continued down the sidewalk. When he saw Liz, Jackson waved and headed in her direction.

"How's rehearsal?"

"I don't want to talk about it."

He looked concerned. "That bad?"

"I know not to leave my day job."

"Sorry. If it helps, I appreciate all the work that is going into the reenactment."

"I'll be fine once Heritage Day is over." She nodded down the street. "How about you? Late meeting?"

"Remember the replacement building markers I was telling you about?"

She nodded.

"We've been getting some pushback from some of the residents. They don't like any of the name changes we've proposed."

"Which means?"

"The project is on hold right now, except for the courthouse lobby, which we've already renamed to showcase the historical artifacts Bert has collected. The new name will be a surprise."

"This event isn't going smoothly for anyone."

"I thought the committee was all in, but then Thomas Sullivan started making a racket. The Sullivan Ironworks placed a bid to cast new markers, which we turned down."

"He couldn't have liked that decision."

"It was only practical. Iron markers are too heavy and costly to make. We're better off with lightweight aluminum." He stuffed his hands in his pockets. "But enough about my meeting."

"Does Mr. Sullivan always cause problems for you?"

"Not every time. Why?"

"It seems like his name keeps coming up. Lilith Granger's too."

"They are descendants of the town forefathers."

"I know. But why not embrace the celebration? They both seem to be bitter about it."

"Maybe they want more recognition?"

"No, I don't think that's it. I guess I'm surprised they aren't more excited about the celebration like the rest of the town seems to be."

"Their families have been involved in one way or another over the years. Maybe it's old hat to them now."

"Then I guess Thomas wouldn't care about the marker changes."

"He only brought up a few drawbacks that any council person might think of, and we listened to his considerations."

"Such as?"

"Public perspective on the name changes. Some argue that we should leave history alone in light of the actions of the history thief. Others are more worried about the cost. Normal concerns, mostly. Sullivan tried to convince us to reconsider the iron markers, but finances won that argument." Fatigue laced his voice. "I doubt we'll solve the problems tonight, Liz. Whoever is staging these thefts has backed us into a tight corner. But changing the building markers will be tabled for a later date."

Liz glanced at the theater doors. "I should get back inside."

"The show must go on." He smiled, though it was clear the recent strain was taking its toll.

She smiled back. "Right. Talk to you later."

Before she reentered the playhouse, Liz looked over her shoulder. Jackson was walking to his truck and the only person in sight, but she still had the distinct feeling she was being watched. She shivered and went inside.

After the fittings, the actors ran through the scene one last time. While it wasn't perfect, it was the best Liz could expect after such a disorganized beginning. She dismissed the group, then helped Mary Ann, Sadie, and Amber tidy up the costume racks.

Sadie draped dresses on hangers. "You know, this reenactment could be the beginning of something big." She held up her hand when Liz started to protest. "Amber has an idea for a play featuring the events that have transpired these last few weeks. And just think, we'll have to wait until Heritage Day to find out the conclusion."

"How about a happy ending: tourists having a wonderful day with no excitement except for the reenactment?" Mary Ann said, her expression hopeful.

Sadie snorted. "Like that's going to happen."

"I have to say, I can't wait for the outcome." Amber nearly danced on tiptoes. "These situations are fodder for great stories. As I've been working on the script, the words have been flowing. I almost feel guilty saying this, but I want to thank the thief for setting up this story for me." She stopped. Her face colored at the other women's shocked expressions. "Not me, specifically, but for the sake of the events he set in motion. I'll be disappointed if nothing exciting happens at the celebration . . ." She paused and added quickly, "From a writer's perspective."

"I don't think the thief will go easy on us," Sadie said. "He hasn't so far."

"I have to agree with Sadie," Amber said. "Until Saturday we have to play along. Oh, *play* along. Get it?"

Only Sadie and Amber laughed.

The women cleaned up, got the costumes back to the storage room, and headed home for the night.

Instead of going right to bed, Liz spread out the notes she'd gathered so far on the dining room table when she returned to the inn. With a legal pad nearby, she jotted down references to Heritage Day:

–Celebration was to be funded by town.

–Heritage Day would stay on the calendar unless changes were necessary.

–The families of those who participated would be honored.

She continued reading and came upon an additional document from a town council meeting six months prior to this year's Heritage Day. It contradicted, but didn't entirely negate, one of the original Heritage Day requirements. "As of this year, focus of Pleasant Creek Heritage Day will be less on individual family recognition and more on the town as a whole. Money has been put aside for the marker refurbishing, with the recommendation of merging existing historical landmark names with current locations, a mixing of the old and new."

A subcommittee had been formed to check into the cost, which included bids for the marker replacements.

She sat back.

Jackson had said the entire committee hadn't agreed on the marker updates yet. Thomas Sullivan had concerns, but hadn't come right out and opposed the project. He had even proposed that the markers be made by Sullivan Ironworks; he couldn't have been happy to have lost the bid.

But what about Lilith? It didn't appear that she was as tuned into government affairs. Still, word of the changes might have trickled back to her. She already had a chip on her shoulder. Could the loss of recognition for both her and her deceased husband's families have pushed her over the edge?

There was only one way to find out. She needed to visit Thomas and Lilith again and ask probing questions. She hoped she'd get some answers, because right now, these two were in the spotlight.

"And then the men toppled over, just like dominoes."

Edna regaled Liz's breakfast guests the next morning with stories about the reenactment rehearsal. Liz cringed every time Edna mentioned how things had gone wrong, which seemed to be most of the time. While the group laughed good-naturedly and enjoyed Liz's summer vegetable egg scramble, she kept busy so she wouldn't hear the conversation, however well-intentioned the participants were. "Liz is doing a great job, but these things happen," Edna said. "It's all part of the fun."

Liz might have agreed, if there weren't so much at stake.

As Liz went into the kitchen to fill another platter, Beans let out a loud woof. She stopped and looked at his empty bowl.

"Sorry, buddy. My mind is elsewhere this morning." Nearly tripping over the dog as he followed her to the kibble, she said, "Patience, Beans. Here you go." She poured the food and the dog descended on it like he was starving. One only had to look at him to know that wasn't the case. "Enjoy," she said, then hustled about the kitchen.

Minutes later, Liz heard a knock at the utility room door. When she got there, to her surprise, Miriam stood outside, a frown marring her pretty face. She handed Liz a newspaper.

"Have you seen the headline today?"

Liz led her into the kitchen and then took the paper. The headline read: "Heritage Day Reenactment Disaster." She saw that the story was filed by Rob Carver.

Her eyes grew wide. "Is he serious?"

It was just like him to shoot off like a loose cannon, even after he'd insisted he wanted them to work together.

Liz read the details and then said, "It was practice. An early practice at that." She glanced up at Miriam. "I never even saw him at the theater."

Miriam pointed to the paper. "According to the story, he snuck in last night. He must have sat in the back row and observed when you had your hands full."

I wouldn't put it past him to have been the one skulking around the theater on Saturday too. "So now he's sunk to humiliating people?" Liz held up the paper. "My name is plastered all over the front page."

"He does not seem to care."

Suddenly a thought occurred to Liz. "Are you teaching a class today?"

"No. I came to town with Philip and saw the newspaper in front of the market. Sarah told me how booked the inn has been, so I thought you might not have had a chance to see the headline. I hoped to warn you before your guests saw it."

"Is that why you came to the utility room door?"

"Ja. Also, I must speak to Sarah."

"Let me call her."

Miriam placed a hand on Liz's arm as she passed. "Is the article true? Is the reenactment going badly?"

Liz crumpled the paper in her hand. "Afraid so. This history thief knows he has us running scared. We jump through hoops and he's happy. My concern is, what if someone gets hurt because the reenactment doesn't meet his expectations? Then I've failed. Angry people aren't reasonable."

"So far he has been very calculating. Like brazenly taking Philip's Werkzeugs out of the wagon." She shivered. "Even though we were the only Amish family personally affected, people in our community are troubled."

"I'm sorry this ugliness has reached you."

"We have prayed this person would stop. Philip wants us to stay away from Heritage Day, but we have put so much work into the goods we are selling."

"As have the other merchants in town. Jackson, Chief Houghton, and Sadie have been threatened, yet they're not hiding in fear. I'm doing my best to follow their example by organizing this reenactment. I'm just hoping I won't make things worse. We all have to work together and hope for the best."

"Which is the other reason I am here. I wanted to let Sarah know I picked up the supplies we needed so she does not have to stop on her way home."

"Always looking out for others."

A blush stained Miriam's cheeks. "That's what family does."

Liz hugged her cousin. "Thanks for the heads-up. None of my guests have read the paper or I would have heard about it by now."

"Philip suggested I come see you since you are now in the forefront. We worry."

Oh Miriam, if you only knew. Liz thought again of the intimidating anonymous note left on her doorstep, but she didn't want to worry her gentle-hearted relative with the details.

"You are family," Miriam said.

At those words, Liz's chest expanded. "Family who might be in trouble." She held up the newspaper. "Rob is taking a risk by writing these articles. He's adding fuel to an already burning fire."

Miriam's words were subdued when she said, "Perhaps he hopes that by publishing his story, the thief will be goaded into making a mistake."

The best-laid plans, Liz thought, hoping Rob's plan didn't blow up in their faces.

15

Liz had just seen Miriam to the door after she spoke to Sarah when her cell phone rang. She answered, surprised to hear Bert on the other end.

"I'm sorry to bother you, but I just had a visitor."

Liz couldn't deny her curiosity. "Don't keep me in suspense."

He chuckled. "Lilith Granger."

"Now that's a surprise."

"She stopped by to donate a piece of history for the exhibit. A silver bell."

"Just like the one I saw in her purse."

"When I opened up this morning, she was on the doorstep waiting. Said she wanted to make a donation before she changed her mind."

"Odd."

"Lilith was skittish, to say the least. Dropped off her bell and left."

Why would she donate it now and not the day Liz ran into her?

"I don't think Lilith's visit has anything to do with the thefts, but I thought you might like to know since you were asking about her."

Why would he think Lilith had nothing to do with the thefts? Because he was the culprit? "Thanks, Bert."

She hung up, more baffled than ever. What was Lilith's game? Liz went to the dining room and motioned to Sarah. "I'll be back in a few minutes."

Sarah nodded and Liz quickly made her way to Sew Welcome. The doors had just opened, and Sadie and Mary Ann were by the counter, preparing to start the day.

"Quick question, Sadie. You mentioned you used to have tea parties with Lilith's mother's silver tea set. Did the bell have any significance?"

"Not that I can recall. We used it to play games and such. Why?"

"Lilith just donated it to Bert's collection."

Sadie's mouth opened and closed. "Happy memories are the only reason it would mean much to Lilith, as far as I know." She paused. "She donated it?"

"Yes. Which is strange since Bert said she wanted to leave it before she changed her mind."

"I can't believe she followed through," Sadie murmured. "And why the bell?"

"Your friendship goes back a long time. Perhaps there's more history to the bell than you remember," Mary Ann reasoned.

"After I clean up the breakfast dishes, let's take a drive back to Lilith's house and get to the bottom of this once and for all."

Sadie, her expression confused, nodded.

"I'll be back to get you."

The remainder of breakfast time dragged on, but soon the guests were either in their rooms or in town for the day. Liz finished cleaning up and hung her apron in the kitchen, then grabbed her purse and went to get Sadie.

Minutes later, they were back on the same route they'd taken previously to Lilith's house. Liz guided the car carefully around the craters in the road. Lilith's run-down car was parked in the driveway.

Sadie leaned forward to peer out the windshield. "She's home."

"But will she speak to us?"

"She will."

After parking, they made their way to the front door. This time, Liz paid better attention to her surroundings. The house seemed even shabbier than she'd noticed last time. A small crack ran along the edge of a window. Rotted pieces of shingle showed in numerous places.

Liz rang the doorbell while Sadie stood front and center, waiting to face her old friend. Unlike the last visit, the door opened quickly. Lilith peered outside, her face drawn, her hair pulled up into its customary messy bun.

"We'd like to speak to you," Sadie said in the tone she reserved for serious business.

Lilith flinched, glanced at Liz, and then opened the door to let the women enter. In the hallway, Lilith said, "Let's go into the parlor."

As she led the way, Liz couldn't help but see that the inside of the house was no better off than the outside. The wallpaper in the foyer had faded so that Liz could barely make out the pattern. The wood floors were scuffed, but clean, and covered with threadbare throw rugs. As Lilith waved an arm in the direction of the sofa, Liz noticed the fabric had been repaired in multiple places.

Sadie sank down onto the sofa, her sigh heavy as she looked at Lilith, who had taken a seat in an armchair. "Lilith, what is going on?"

Lilith's eyes were bright. She looked about to argue, until her shoulders drooped and she slumped into the chair. "I . . . did something I regret."

"Haven't we all?" Sadie said.

At the gentle words, Lilith straightened. "I thought I was making a point, but now . . ."

"Does this have anything to do with the bell you donated to Bert?" Sadie asked.

Lilith's head lifted sharply. "How do you know about that?"

"Bert told me," Liz said, keeping to the stern tone Sadie had established.

Lilith picked at a thread on her skirt. "You don't remember, do you?"

"I've been racking my brain," Sadie answered.

"We were here playing with the tea set, like we always did. That day, Mother had brewed tea and it was more than just make-believe. We were going to have a real party."

Sadie perked up. "Yes. She said she was going to make the day special. She laid out the cream and sugar, just like she did for the adults."

"She handed me the bell. She told me to ring it to summon her."

"We started playing with it, ringing every few minutes." Sadie smiled. "Your mother was such a good sport. She'd come in and say, 'You rang?' and we'd dissolve into giggles."

"She told us something very important that day. Something I refused to take into account these many years later." She closed her eyes. "Mother said friends were as precious as silver and gold. She said I should never take for granted the friendship I had with you, Sadie." Lilith swallowed a sob. "I was angry, and I let that emotion take over, tossing aside the years of happy memories we shared."

Sadie rose and moved to her friend's side, taking Lilith's hand in her own. Lilith's eyes flew open. "We both forgot what your kind, loving mother told us. Do you think enough time has gone by to finally put those wise words into action?"

Lilith sniffled. Nodded.

"Is that why you brought the bell to Bert? To let go of the bitterness of the lost friendship?" Liz asked.

"Yes." Lilith's voice was thick. "When you showed up on my front porch, the resentment I'd let build up for years made me slam the door on a second chance. I thought showing my anger was my chance to shove the loss of our friendship in your face. After you left, I recognized I was empty inside. I realized too late that I wanted to make amends. The bell was symbolic. If I could get Bert to display it, and you saw it, then maybe I had a chance at restoring our friendship."

Tears were running down both women's faces. Liz looked around for a tissue box but didn't see one in the parlor.

"In the kitchen." Lilith pointed down the hallway.

Jumping up, Liz found her way to a very large, very outdated kitchen. The appliances were dull, the linoleum floor yellow with age. The windows in the kitchen were open. Bleached cotton curtains fluttered in the breeze. She searched the countertops for tissues, finding none. Looking around, she noticed a box on the large farmhouse table.

As she crossed the room, a faint whiff of smoke prickled her nose. Alarmed, she walked to the stove, but the burners were off. She spun around, scanning the room. Nothing appeared out of the ordinary. The scent grew stronger. Looking out the window, she saw a trail of gray smoke floating into the blue sky from a barn out back.

"Sadie! Lilith! You need to come in here. Fast!"

Moments later footsteps hurried down the hall, and then the women were crossing the linoleum to join her. By now, Liz had the door open. "It looks like there's a fire in your barn."

"What?" Lilith moved to the door, a small cry escaping her when she saw the column of smoke.

Liz had already found a phone mounted on the wall. She quickly called 911. After speaking to the operator, she stepped onto the small stoop out back with the others.

"I never should have kept it," Lilith moaned. "Look what I've done."

Before Liz could ask what Lilith meant, licks of fire appeared around the edges of the building. Lilith starting sprinting to the barn with surprising speed. Liz gasped and followed, trying to stop the older woman. She grabbed hold of Lilith's shoulder, but Lilith shrugged off Liz's hold and kept moving.

Liz tried grabbing for Lilith again, but Lilith dodged her just as they reached the wooden structure. The heavy fumes and heat were overwhelming. Liz firmly took hold of Lilith's arm, intending to pull her back, but Lilith swiveled and, with two hands, pushed Liz away.

Liz regained her balance and went after Lilith as the older woman fumbled with the latch. Suddenly the doors opened wide. Lilith rushed inside the hazy interior.

"Lilith, no!" Liz screamed.

As Liz dashed toward the door of the barn to see if she could safely catch Lilith, she heard sirens in the distance. Help was on the way. She should have been relieved, but one look inside the barn made her heart pound like crazy. The smoke was so heavy it completely obscured her already blurry vision. Coughing and blinking through watering eyes, Liz could barely make out Lilith's form in the center of the barn. Lilith ran across Liz's line of vision and toward one wall. The crazy woman was yanking at something, but spasms of coughing overpowered her. Lilith doubled over, regained her composure, and tried again. Liz saw her chance, held her breath, and raced toward Lilith. She grabbed the woman's arms and began to forcibly drag her into the sunshine.

Still fighting, Lilith broke loose. Liz lost sight of her. Covering her nose and mouth with her shirt, Liz moved a little deeper into the distorted gloom when suddenly Lilith passed by, dragging something large behind her. Just before reaching the doors, another coughing spell halted Lilith's progress. She dropped the item and Liz swooped in to push Lilith outside. They both fell to the ground, coughing while simultaneously trying to suck in air. A grimy coating of ash caked Liz's throat. Her skin felt hot and sticky.

A fire truck rounded the house and came to a stop only feet from where they lay. Firefighters dressed in bunker gear and heavy boots got to work, grabbing hoses and dragging them closer to the flames. Someone cleared the perimeter. The crackling roar of the fire seemed to grow louder in her ears. A voice shouted for the women to move back.

Taking Lilith's arm, Liz tugged her up and moved her to safety. They were both covered in soot and ash, but in one piece. As they grew close to Sadie, she wrapped her arms around Lilith. Liz bent over, hands on her knees, trying to take deep breaths, but with her throat so scratchy and her eyes stinging, she only succeeded in setting off another coughing jag.

The steady hum of the fire engine and shouting voices deadened in Liz's ears. She blinked, dazed for a moment, surprised to find an ambulance so close. Hadn't she moved? And why was it so hard to breathe?

Her sight grew dim and before she had a chance to topple over, strong hands grabbed hold of her and led her to the ambulance. There, someone spoke to her, but Liz couldn't make out the words. As her heart beat too fast, she sank to the ground. The paramedic crouched beside her, taking her pulse.

He checked her airway, then placed an oxygen mask over her nose and mouth. At first she gulped too much air and grew dizzy, but the man gently instructed her to slow her breathing and soon the flow of oxygen revived her.

Then he checked her hands. "No burns." He flipped her hands over, tugging off the rings she wore on either hand. "Looking for swelling," he explained. After his examination, he gently set her hands back into her lap.

The longer she sat, the more surreal and frightening the scene before her became. The flames seemed to be under control, but the back part of the barn collapsed with a loud crash. Liz shuddered. They might have been inside when it fell because of Lilith's insane sprint into the flames. What was she thinking to run into the burning structure? And what on earth had Liz been thinking to follow?

"Liz." Sadie's worried face came into view. Liz nodded to assure her friend she'd be okay. Right now, her throat wasn't up to speaking.

Chaos reigned in the yard. Liz didn't know how long men tromped through the partially destroyed barn, but finally the pumps turned off, the silence deafening after all the racket. The sad building dripped water and soot. Fortunately, the fire had been contained and hadn't spread to the grass or outlying areas. The barn might be history, but at least Lilith's home was safe.

The EMT spoke to Liz again and checked her vitals. Liz removed the mask, relieved to be able to breathe on her own, even though her throat burned. The young man pronounced her free to go. She wasn't going anywhere until she knew Lilith was okay.

She made her way on shaky legs to Sadie and asked in a raspy voice, "How is she?"

"About the same as you, but it looks like she'll be fine. The young man didn't think she needed to make a trip to the hospital."

Liz gazed at the barn. "What was so important that she risked her life for it?"

"We'll have to wait until she gets her voice back to answer that question."

By now, Chief Houghton had arrived. He walked the women back to the house. "Once you ladies can speak, I'll be needing some answers."

Sadie filled glasses with cold water, handing one to a grateful Liz. She sipped, nearly crying when the cool liquid soothed her throat. She plopped down in a chair by the kitchen table while Lilith did the same. Moments passed as they drank.

"Want to explain what that stunt was about?" the chief asked, his eyes dark.

Lilith opened her mouth to explain, but coughed instead.

"When she saw the barn on fire, she ran toward it," Liz croaked, her hoarse voice barely audible. "It looked like she was trying to remove something from inside."

Lilith nodded. She grabbed a tissue from the box, wiped her eyes, and then twisted the tissue in her fingers.

"I can't fathom what could be in that barn that is so important that you should risk your life," the chief said.

Tears streaked down Lilith's sooty cheeks.

Sadie came up beside him and placed her hand on his arm. "Can the questions wait? They've been through an ordeal and aren't going anywhere."

He looked back at the women and nodded, then stepped outside to speak to the fire chief.

"I'd also like to know, Lilith." Liz coughed, her throat still tight and raspy. "What was so important you needed to save?"

"I told you I was guilty," came her husky reply.

"Of what?" Sadie urged.

Lilith tossed her tissue on the table and rose. She wrapped her arms around her middle as she walked to a window and peered outside. "You're going to be angry with me."

Sadie joined her, Liz on her heels. "Lilith, you're scaring me. What did you want to save?"

Lilith glanced out the window again and her breath caught in her throat. Liz craned her neck to see what was going on.

One of the firefighters rolled a circular object from the structure. He dropped it on the grass and went back to the opening. Lilith let out a sharp cry.

"What is it?" Liz asked.

"The wagon wheel." She glanced over her shoulder at Sadie and Liz. "It's been in my barn."

16

Liz lowered herself into a nearby chair. "The wagon wheel? From in front of the courthouse?"

Sadie blinked. "But how?"

"Someone must have dropped it off here at night. I never heard a thing. I went out there for a garden tool a week or so ago, and there it sat, dead center on the barn floor."

"But why would someone bring it here?"

Lilith motioned for Sadie to sit then pulled out a chair of her own. She took a sip of water before she spoke again. "I deserved it." She sighed. "I didn't tell you, but I overheard Wanda Reese talking about the historical society donations one day when I was at the grocery store. I already knew about the drive for family donations before the letters went out."

Sadie's face grew grim. "Wanda sure can talk."

"I was excited. I started thinking about what I could donate. I have many Granger and French heirlooms, and since Heritage Day is coming up, I was sure I could find the perfect piece. Only the letter never came. I felt slighted." She met Sadie's steady gaze. "How could you leave me out?"

"It was an oversight. And you know Wanda's not the most organized woman in the world."

Lilith shrugged. "I didn't see it that way."

"You thought I deliberately left you off the list?"

"Yes."

Sadie sat back in the chair. "I don't suppose I've given you any reason to think anything but the worst. If I'd been in your shoes, I might have felt the same."

Liz rested her elbows on the table. "So, the wagon wheel?"

"When I discovered it here, I tried to hide it. Darned thing fell over even when I tried to lean it against the wall."

"Why didn't you report it?"

Lilith lowered her eyes. "I hadn't gotten that far ahead. After the shock of finding it, I was rather glad people would be missing it. I thought the wheel going missing could be my way of sticking it to the historical society."

Sadie asked the question hanging in the air. "Lilith, are you the history thief?"

"No." She dragged her hands down her face. "I swear I didn't steal anything. Just when I decided to call the chief, the reports of the other thefts in town started."

"You do realize it will look bad for you," Liz said, "when everyone hears you've had the wagon wheel on your premises."

"Someone is framing me. I never touched the other stolen goods."

"The chief is going to want proof."

"Then he can search my house. He won't find anything."

Sadie rose, took a few steps, and turned. "Lilith, what's really going on here?"

Lilith pressed her lips together.

"It's more than a perceived slight, isn't it? And it's more than being worried what people will think if they find out you have the wheel."

Tears leaked down her cheeks again. Her skin sagged and her shoulders suddenly looked like she carried the weight of the world. "You're going to find out anyway."

Liz glanced at Sadie, who raised her brows as if to say, *now what*?

"I've been shoplifting," Lilith said in a small voice.

Liz shook her head, dumbfounded.

Lilith waved her hand in the air. "As you can see, I can't keep up with this place. I try, but what little money I have doesn't go far. So I started taking things, just little things like soap and toothpaste. The more I got away with it, the more I took. Canned foods. Produce." Her breath hitched. "I'm so ashamed."

"Why haven't you asked for some assistance?" Sadie pressed.

"You know as well as anyone how proud I am. I got in too deep. Then the thefts started around town. I knew I had to keep quiet or expose my shame."

"Oh, Lilith."

"I suppose the truth will come out now."

"I don't see how it can remain a secret."

Liz rested her elbows on the table. "Sadie mentioned you have children. Can't they help?"

"They have their own lives in Seattle and Virginia Beach. Raising children of their own has kept them busy. They pay for my trips to visit them, to lend a helping hand with the grandchildren or join them on family vacations. They never come here."

Sadie's cheeks grew red. "Lilith Granger, if the kids knew just how far into disrepair this place had fallen, they'd be horrified."

"I just didn't want to be a bother. And then when the place got worse, I knew they'd be upset that I didn't call to begin with."

Liz's heart squeezed tight. By not wanting to burden her children, Lilith hadn't given them the chance to support their mother. How alike she and Sadie were, determined to live alone and take care of themselves when they had plenty of people who loved them and would help at a moment's notice. Only Sadie hadn't allowed bitterness and old wounds to keep her from accepting the love and friendship of the people around her.

"Everyone is going to think I stole their belongings," Lilith said again. Where before embarrassment shadowed her eyes, fear took its place.

"They will. Until we straighten out this mess," Sadie said.

"Which starts with telling the chief." Liz rose and went to the door. She waited until she caught the chief's eye and waved him back to the house.

"I'm with you," Sadie guaranteed her friend. "You won't go through this alone."

Moments later the chief appeared, stomping his boots on the mat before entering the kitchen.

"Care to explain why the missing courthouse wagon wheel is lying in your yard?"

Sadie nodded at Lilith.

"Someone put it in my barn."

"And you didn't know?"

Lilith hesitated, then said, "I did know."

"Why didn't you call me?"

Lilith worried her lower lip.

The chief let out a long breath. "And the other stolen belongings?"

"I don't have them."

"Under the circumstances, I'm going to have to search the premises."

After Lilith gave her permission for the search, the chief called the station and asked for another officer to meet him, then continued to take the women's statements. At one point, Liz pulled him aside.

"Do you have any idea what caused the fire?"

"This is an ongoing investigation."

"Yes, but now that we know the wheel was inside, it is suspicious. A barn just doesn't catch on fire without a reason."

He sent her a stern look. "The fire marshal will do his job and come up with answers."

Liz glanced over her shoulder at Lilith. "We can't leave her here alone."

"My suggestion would also be that Mrs. Granger spend a few days elsewhere. She's pretty shaken up."

"I'll see what I can do."

While the chief spoke to Lilith, Liz cornered Sadie. "Lilith shouldn't be alone."

"When the chief says we can go, I'm taking her to my house. We're long overdue for a serious conversation."

"You're always ahead of the curve."

Sadie smiled, but without the customary twinkle in her eyes. "Unfortunately, I didn't see this coming. If Lilith had been here alone, she might have been killed."

"That thought occurred to me."

"We'll both rest easier at my house."

"See if you can find out if anything else has roused her suspicions lately."

"I will. And you?"

"A long, hot shower is calling my name." Liz's clothes reeked of smoke, and the stench had taken up permanent residence in her nose. She would need extra-strength floral body wash to counteract the lingering effects of the afternoon's events.

When the other officer arrived, he and the chief conducted a sweeping search of the house. An hour later, they came up empty. No stolen items. Lilith was not the history thief. Or if she was, the items were not on her property.

"One more thing, ladies. Please don't mention the wagon wheel to the general public. For now, I don't want the thief to know we have it."

Liz shuddered to think that whoever had stolen the past might still be at large, with the future of the town in his hands.

After a soothing shower to remove the odor of scorched wood from her hair and skin, Liz felt marginally better. Her hands were still a tad shaky and her throat scratchy. The aftereffects were starting to catch up with her.

Intending to make a light dinner and retire early, Liz found her plans changed when the Material Girls showed up, serving dishes in hand. They immediately took over the kitchen.

"Mac and cheese," Caitlyn announced as she placed her dish on the counter. When she removed the top, a cheesy aroma filled the room. "If anything calls for comfort food, almost being trapped in a fire is it."

Despite the events of the day, Liz's stomach rumbled.

Opal uncovered her bowl. "Tomato and cucumber salad. Fresh from my garden."

"Brownies," Naomi said. "Tonight also calls for chocolate. Lots of it."

"Is Sadie coming?" Caitlyn asked as she removed plates from the cupboard.

"Not tonight," Mary Ann answered. "I talked to her a little while ago. She and Lilith are exhausted, so they're going to stay in tonight. Maybe they can catch up and make amends. I closed the store early, just in case you needed anything, Liz."

Liz filled the teakettle. "Company is the best medicine." Friendship and a bracing cup of tea now sounded like the perfect antidote to her trying day.

Soon, dishes were filled and the ladies took seats around the table, ready for an update.

"How in the world did you end up in a burning barn?" Mary Ann asked.

Liz related the story of running after Lilith. "I didn't think I'd ever get her out of there. She's extremely strong. And stubborn."

"You'd think she'd know better." Opal *tsked*. "What was she thinking?"

Liz waited until all eyes were on her. "She was thinking she needed to remove the stolen wagon wheel before it went up in flames."

A brief silence ensued before questions volleyed her way again. She raised her hand. "No, I'm convinced Lilith is not the history thief. The chief searched her residence and no stolen belongings were found. She swears someone deliberately put the wheel in her barn without her knowledge."

"Good heavens," Mary Ann said. "Why?"

"To frame her. It almost worked too."

"Then who is the thief?" Naomi asked.

"We still don't know. I have to admit I was seriously looking at Lilith, but now . . ." Liz shrugged.

Caitlyn scooped up a bite of macaroni. "Doesn't the chief have any leads?"

"Not that he's sharing. To be honest, I think he's as stumped as everyone else. Oh, he asked that we keep the news of the wheel quiet for now. But I know I can trust you."

The women nodded.

"What about Bert?" Opal broke off a piece of crusty bread. "Does he have any thoughts?"

Liz glanced at Mary Ann before giving her opinion. "He might be the thief."

Silence filled the room.

Opal spoke first. "Come again?"

Liz told them about the knife in her tire being traced back to him.

"And you think you know people," Opal huffed.

"The chief hasn't made an arrest, so the investigation is still ongoing. Amber Pierce has motive too. She could be staging this entire thing to try to drum up publicity for the playhouse," Liz said.

A frown wrinkled Mary Ann's forehead. "Don't forget Rob Carver doing enough speculation for everyone. His latest story was outrageous."

"I think *he* thinks he's helping," Liz said, amazed she was standing up for the overzealous reporter. "He's using the paper to incite the culprit, to goad him or her into making a wrong move, even if it's for his own selfish reasons."

"Your rehearsal wasn't that awful," Mary Ann stated.

Liz chuckled, touched by her friend's loyalty. "It was. I can laugh now, but the other night?" She rubbed her temple. "I'm getting a headache just thinking about it."

Mary Ann passed the salad around the table. "Jackson owes you. Big time."

"I was the one who offered, so he's off the hook."

The remainder of the meal consisted of chitchat, the topic of the history thief mercifully dropped. Before long, plates were emptied and the brownies had disappeared. But even the chocolate dessert didn't lift their moods.

Liz tried to stifle her yawns, but after the fifth try, she gave up.

"I think we'd better get a move on, girls," Mary Ann suggested as she rose and started collecting dirty dishes. "Liz is bushed and has to be up early tomorrow to serve breakfast."

"And feed Edna Hastings's unquenchable curiosity," Liz said. "I'll be answering her questions all morning."

Working together, they had the kitchen tidied up in no time. Each gave Liz a hug as they took their leave. Only Mary Ann hung around.

"Are you sure you're going to be okay?"

"Once my head hits the pillow I'll be asleep, I promise."

"Call me if you need anything."

Liz smiled and saw her friend out the front door. She'd just reached her quarters when the doorbell rang. Thinking one of the women had forgotten something, she was surprised to find Jackson standing under the porch light.

"Is something wrong?" she asked as she opened the door.

"Not exactly." His dark expression made her nervous. "Mind if I come in?"

She stepped back and Jackson entered. Even in the dim light, she couldn't miss the circles under his eyes. The thefts, threats, and inability to uncover the identity of the thief were taking their toll on everyone, the mayor most of all.

"I heard about the fire. The chief assured me you're okay, but I wanted to check for myself."

"It was a little tense there for a while, but I'm fine."

He let out a heavy breath. "Good."

"Do you want to sit down?"

"No, I won't stay long. I wanted to see you and also bring you the latest news."

"You mean there's more news than the fire?"

He nodded. "A call came into the town hall. The caller was trying to reach my office but got my assistant instead. The history thief has a new message for us."

"Oh boy. Maybe I should sit down."

Jackson wrapped his warm hand around her suddenly chilly arm to keep her steady. His worried gaze met hers. If she had to hear bad news from anyone, she'd want it to come from Jackson, because she knew that along with the news, he'd do everything in his power to keep her and the town safe. With that assurance, she stood straight.

"What's the message?"

"The thief said that today's fireworks are nothing like those in store for the town on Heritage Day."

"Did the voice belong to a man or woman?"

"Hard to tell. It was digitally modified. The chief is running the call."

Liz knew that would probably lead to a prepaid, so-called "burner phone." With so little information, they would have no way to prepare for the full explosion of the thief's plan.

She met Jackson's gaze. "So now we have to look over our shoulders on Saturday to make sure no one tries to outdo a burning barn?"

"That's the impression I got."

"Then let's hope that the history thief never gets a chance to perform the grand finale."

17

"Very good job, everyone."

Thursday night was the last opportunity the actors had to rehearse until the reenactment on Saturday afternoon. The first run went smoothly, but Liz couldn't control the butterflies in her stomach. Ever since the fire, she'd been on edge, waiting for the history thief to strike again. The feeling of being watched had intensified by the day.

Mary Ann and Sadie had come along in case there were any last-minute costume alterations. The teens from the Sew Welcome class had repaired the costumes that afternoon, but there was always the chance more stitching would be required. Sadie hadn't said much about Lilith, and Liz decided it was best not to pry as the two of them worked out their past differences.

As the cast and crew were getting ready to run through the scene one final time, a ruckus came from the lobby, followed by a big man entering the theater from the back. Thomas Sullivan rolled a large wheel down the aisle. He reached the front of the theater and sought out Liz.

"My wife said you could use this replica."

"Yes, thanks, Mr. Sullivan." Liz smiled. "I wasn't sure if you were interested in the reenactment."

"My wife likes this acting stuff so I wanted to lend a hand."

Maybe he isn't such an old grouch after all. "So you just happened to have an old wagon wheel lying around?"

"Got lots of stuff in my workshop." He glanced around. "Where do you want it?"

"How about in front of the signing table?"

Thomas wheeled it over. "Maybe on the side here?"

"No. In front. The centerpiece."

Thomas scowled but placed it in the center.

Liz had the actors get in place to start the scene. When Kendell as Mayor French spoke to the townspeople from his place on the far right of the table, Thomas cut in.

"He should be more to the left."

"I think he's fine," Liz said.

"But more to the left is historically accurate."

"According to my research, no one knows for sure where anyone stood so I think we're okay." Liz struggled to tamp down her annoyance. Directing the reenactment was stressful enough without anyone else trying to take over.

Claire hurried to her husband's side. "It's fine, dear. Don't make a fuss."

"And I appreciate your insight, Mr. Sullivan," Liz quickly added, "but we're going to stick with what we've already rehearsed for simplicity's sake."

Thomas crossed his thick arms over his barrel chest. "Makes sense, I guess."

Claire pushed him toward the front row. "Why don't you take a seat?"

"Nah. I'll leave you actors to it." He gave his wife a one-armed hug and left.

Relieved to have control again, Liz turned to face the cast. "Back to the top, Kendell."

They went through the scene again, this time without mishaps. Liz applauded the group of actors. "You guys are awesome."

"Why wouldn't we be?" Kendell asked. "We are professionals."

"It shows. Now, I think we can call it a day. Great job, everyone."

Soon after the crowd began to disperse. Liz spoke to a few actors asking last-minute questions, but she felt good about the day's progress.

She only hoped the history thief would approve.

"No pressure," she muttered to herself.

Dropping her pen and paper in her tote, Liz looked up to see Claire Sullivan coming her way. She steeled herself for more Sullivan suggestions.

"Liz, I wanted to apologize about my husband's comments tonight. He tends to be a tad outspoken."

"It's okay. I'm happy he was able to find a wheel on such short notice."

"He's been working on fixing it up for a while."

"Really? I guess since the original is missing, we were fortunate he had this wheel at home."

"It's one of his little projects. He keeps himself busy. Even though he retired from the ironworks, he's still involved with the business in an advisory capacity. Most days he likes to putter in the workshop and keep his hand in old hobbies."

"Good for him. I imagine when you've worked all your life retirement can be difficult to get used to."

"He's managing."

"What does he think of the thefts in town?"

"Frankly, he's amazed by how easily people let their things be stolen."

Let? Liz tilted her head in surprise. "You didn't have anything taken from your house?"

"Heavens, no. Thomas is very careful."

Liz doubted Thomas Sullivan would overlook a theft on his property.

"But we do feel for the folks who had their belongings taken." Claire sent Liz a smile. "Hopefully the thefts are cleared up soon. Good night."

"See you on Heritage Day."

As Amber locked up the theater, she and Kendell asked Liz to join them at The Coffee Cup.

"Why not? I could use a treat," Liz said.

The diner was beginning to slow down for the night when they arrived, but a few customers hung around playing games on tablets or talking on their phones. The scent of coffee had Liz's stomach growling. She'd missed dinner, but fortunately there were a few baked goods in the display case. She ordered a slice of coffee cake along with her latte. She'd never say this aloud, but Naomi's offerings at Sweet Everything were far superior.

After placing their orders, Kendell commandeered a table in the back.

"So," Amber said as they got settled, "we heard about the fire." She shivered. "It must have been frightening."

"It was, but luckily no one was hurt."

"Especially Lilith," Amber continued. "She's such a dear."

Amber and Kendell exchanged glances. Liz wondered what that was about. She didn't have to wait long for her answer.

"It's all over town that Lilith is the history thief," Kendell said. "The rumor is that she set the fire herself and then claimed she was being framed. But people need to get their facts straight."

"What facts?" Liz took a sip of her latte.

"About what Lilith is stealing."

Liz choked. She had no idea Lilith's shoplifting was common knowledge. "Excuse me, what did you say?"

"Lilith. She didn't take our antiques."

"Then what did she take?" Liz tested them, to see what they'd say. The two exchanged puzzled glances.

"Oh dear," Amber said. "We thought you knew."

"That she shoplifts? I just found out." Liz set her cup down. "But you knew?"

"Lilith has experienced a few . . . financial setbacks through the years, so I've heard," Amber went on to say.

"It started at the drugstore," Kendell began. "One day she was there buying some personal items. As I was leaving, I caught her stuffing toothpaste in the bag with her purchases. At first I was shocked. I couldn't believe what I was seeing."

"Didn't you say something? Or call the police?"

"I thought about it, but when I said something to the clerk, she remembered Lilith talking about running short on funds every month. And even though it didn't register at first, I had noticed her appearance growing more and more disheveled. Her clothes were looking worn, and I thought she must not be able to make ends meet."

"One day I happened to mention to Kendell that I thought she lifted some greeting cards we carry in the bookstore," Amber said.

"And then I witnessed her taking canned goods at the grocery store," Kendell added.

Liz broke off a piece of cake. The buttery goodness melted in her mouth, along with the kick of cinnamon. "So you decided to keep quiet?"

"Yes." Kendell took a sip and continued. "All her life, she was something of a Good Samaritan around town. When my daughter was a baby, we had a health scare. Lilith made sure we had meals every night when my wife and I came home from the hospital."

Amber nodded. "And when I first moved to town, she's the one who got me the director position at the playhouse. She didn't participate in the productions any longer, but sensed a kindred spirit and knew I'd take good care of the theater program."

"After all her help, this was our way of giving back to her," Kendell said. "She would never have admitted she needed help, but after we put our stories together, we knew we could repay her by allowing her to keep her dignity. We check in periodically with the places she shops and pay for the items she takes."

Liz felt a surge of love for the town she now called home. These people had seen a need and helped out in their own way, without getting Lilith in trouble or humiliating her. And they'd somehow kept it from Mary Ann and Sadie. Not an easy feat in Pleasant Creek.

"Does the chief know?"

Amber chuckled. "He told us to keep an eye on her and make sure her shoplifting didn't get out of hand, but he didn't want to have to arrest a pillar of the community. We took that as a pass."

"Where is she?" Kendell asked. "My wife called to check on her, but she said the phone just rang and rang."

"She's staying with Sadie."

The pair went silent.

"Yes, I know there's unpleasant history there, but they're working through it."

Amber placed a hand over her chest. "Good, because we're still keeping watch over her."

Liz took another sip, thinking over the new information. "So, if you're sure Lilith didn't take the antiques, do either of you have a theory about who might have done it?"

"At first we thought it might be someone in the historical society," Kendell said, "but since I'm a member, I checked out everyone and no one seemed to have a motive."

"Then we thought maybe Bert recruited someone to take the belongings," Amber shook her head, "but nothing came of it."

"What about the Sullivans?" Liz asked. "They're connected to the charter signing."

"But Thomas loves his family history. He wouldn't tarnish it," Kendell reasoned.

"I see Claire all the time," Amber said. "Why would she participate in the reenactment if her husband was guilty?"

"It was a wild idea," Liz admitted.

"And she's in on the secret about Lilith," Amber added.

"She is?" Liz asked, surprised.

"She mentioned it to me one day when they were in the store together," Amber answered. "Claire hadn't realized I knew about Lilith's shoplifting and vowed to keep the secret."

Amber folded her napkin. "Let's just hope the thief returns everything after the reenactment. I'm still working on my play and can't finish until I know the outcome."

Liz watched Amber as she gathered up their cups to toss into the trash on the way out. Again, Liz was struck by Amber's eagerness to turn the town's distress into a production. She couldn't cross Amber off the suspect list. Not until all of this was over.

By the time Liz got back to the inn, she was exhausted. Less than two days remained until the big event. She still had to get the inn tidied up for the tour, which she'd found out was scheduled late morning to early afternoon. The reenactment would begin at four in the afternoon, leaving folks on edge the entire day, waiting to find out what the history thief had in store for them. So far, Sadie, Jackson, and the chief were safe, but who knew what would happen? Mix in one angry person and a live fireworks display, and there was no telling what kind of explosion would result.

Before going to bed, Liz stopped by the foyer to check on Beans. He snored peacefully in his usual spot. After organizing the ingredients for breakfast in the kitchen, she turned off the lights and made her rounds of the inn, making sure all doors and windows were locked up tight. When she reached the sitting room, something on the coffee table caught her attention.

It was a glossy photo. Had one of her guests left it behind? She took a closer look and gasped. It was a picture of the wagon wheel halfway hidden under a tarp. The photo had apparently been taken in Lilith's barn before it went up in flames.

18

"All the merchants found a copy of the photograph," Chief Houghton told Liz the next morning. "So much for keeping the fact that we found the wagon wheel a secret."

"Why would the thief reveal the location now?"

"To make Lilith look guilty to everyone?" The chief dropped the photo into the empty evidence bag. "I don't expect to find any prints."

"So far the thief has been pretty careful."

"Every one of 'em messes up eventually," he said as he grabbed a muffin on the way out.

Saturday dawned dreary, but as Liz assisted Naomi in the bakery, filling plastic bins to transport the baked goods to her booth, the sun slowly filtered through the cloud cover. The weather report promised a typical hot, sunny summer day, and Liz had her fingers crossed that good weather would hold.

Naomi wiped her hands on her apron and surveyed the bakery. "I think that's everything."

"You certainly didn't skimp. There are more sweets here than I expected."

"This is a big day for sales, but also in terms of my reputation as a baker. Repeat customers are a must, so I need to take advantage of today."

"I understand. Although your everyday foot traffic isn't shabby."

"My clientele is faithful, that's for sure." Naomi chuckled. "I expect my fans from the Senior Center will be out in droves today."

"I think everyone in town will be there."

"Let's get these bins loaded into the van."

Naomi drove the short distance to her booth, parking the van close by. The two quickly unpacked and set up. Naomi fussed over the visual presentation—her trademark coral table coverings and a banner with the bakery logo—while Liz wandered down the street, savoring the images of a small-town Independence Day celebration.

A large banner hung over Main Street, welcoming guests to Pleasant Creek. Red, white, and blue streamers, flags, and other patriotic decorations perked up the merchants' booths. Voices carried as folks readied themselves for the onslaught of tourists who would pack the street in mere hours. Liz couldn't wait for the day to be over, hoping the night's planned fireworks extravaganza would end the revelry on a high note, not in disaster.

Turning back, Liz approached the Sweet Everything booth. "Ready?"

Naomi rummaged through a bag before answering. "I thought I had my sign for the booth."

"I saw it earlier." Liz walked past her friend to dig through another bin carrying different odds and ends Naomi would need during the day. She pulled out the laminated sign. "Here you go."

Blowing out a breath, Naomi flashed Liz a nervous grin. "Thanks. I don't know where my mind is today."

"Focusing on business?"

"And feeling edgy. I keep looking over my shoulder, like I'm waiting for the worst to happen."

"I know what you mean. I woke this morning with a mixture of excitement and dread."

"Are you ready for the tour?"

Liz glanced at her watch. "Mostly. Sarah came in today to get breakfast started, but I need to get back. The tour starts at eleven."

"So I'm guessing we won't see much of each other today?"

"I doubt it. The reenactment is at four, followed by the picnic dinner and softball game at the park."

"Then the fireworks show after dusk."

"So, no, I doubt we'll see each other until later. But if you need help, call my cell."

"Candice and Jenny will be here soon. I'll be fine." Naomi shooed Liz along. "Go. Get ready."

Liz waved. "Have fun."

Naomi chuckled. "You too."

Turning on her heel, Liz started down Main Street toward the inn. Friends and neighbors greeted her along her journey. Most sported happy faces, decked out in their Independence Day best, but as Naomi had mentioned, there was an underlying disquiet. The townspeople knew about the threats, but the tourists did not. Liz hoped it remained that way.

Finally back at the inn, Liz smiled as she walked up the sidewalk, which was lined with small flags. Donald Hastings had volunteered to put them out that morning. The Olde Mansion Inn looked ready for the tour.

To her surprise, Edna greeted her in the foyer, already dressed in her reenactment costume.

"Good morning, Liz."

"You're a little early, don't you think?"

"Excited is more like it. Donald thinks I'm being silly, but I want to get into the part."

"It's supposed to be a hot day, and that fabric doesn't look very breathable."

"Well, when you put it like that . . ."

Liz chuckled. "Why not wear a cooler outfit until the reenactment? You'll be more comfortable. No sense in getting overheated."

"I suppose you're right."

Donald strode out of the dining room. "Another superb breakfast."

"I'm glad you enjoyed it," Liz said.

He glanced at his wife. "I'll be in the four-season room while you get changed. Lots of events today, and we don't want to miss a thing." He headed off to his destination, humming as he went.

"There is nothing worse than when your husband is right, even if he doesn't come out and say it."

"Having never been married, I'll take your word for it."

Edna climbed the stairs to change, and Liz went to the kitchen to find Sarah putting away the leftovers. "Everyone ate already?"

"It was an early crowd. The guests are upstairs getting ready for the celebrations."

"Looks like you have the cleanup well in hand."

"Yes. Once I am finished I must go over to the family booth."

Liz walked back to her quarters and changed into a red-and-white–striped top, navy shorts, and sandals. Adding sparkling earrings and a bracelet, she was ready to host her first tour.

By eleven, only a few visitors had stopped by. Liz shoved down her disappointment until she learned the inn was near to the last stop on the preplanned tour. An hour later, she was busy reciting inn history and handing out her giveaways, pens with the name and number of the inn.

The early afternoon flew by until the final stragglers closed the tour by three. To her delight, she'd made a half dozen future reservations. After a quick sandwich, Liz set off for the courthouse for the reenactment.

The male leads had made sure to get the props delivered to the proper location. At the bottom of the courthouse steps, the men placed an antique table. Matching chairs were set up, the replacement wagon wheel positioned front and center. The sidewalk had been blocked off to make room for the actors, and by three thirty the cast was ready to take the stage.

Liz paced along a small patch of grass in front of the building, her stomach in knots. So far, the events of the day had gone off without a hitch. This reenactment also had to be perfect.

At a quarter to four, Liz joined the actors in the courthouse lobby. The costumed actors in period attire milled around Bert's display cases.

"I hope you don't mind that we took over your exhibit," she told Bert when he came over to greet her.

"Not at all. I've had a busy day so far, and this break is just what I need." His eyes sparkled. "Can you believe all the foot traffic I've had? The history thief has made my display a success."

Amber appeared beside them. "The thief is going to be the main character in my new work. I'm finally going to have a hit play. Thanks, Liz."

"For what?"

"Being a good sport and planning the reenactment."

"This is my one and only directing gig." She pressed her hands on her swirling stomach. "I've never been so nervous."

"I have no doubt this reenactment will go down in history." Bert's face sobered at Liz's discomfort. "In a very positive way."

"Just don't be too critical if it's not one hundred percent accurate."

"No reenactment of another period ever is."

Liz hoped he meant that. As much as she didn't want to believe he was guilty, Bert was still under suspicion. Mary Ann and Sadie showed up as she continued pacing.

"Ladies. Good to see you." She glanced at Mary Ann. "So, how did the pie contest go?"

Sadie beat Mary Ann to the punch. "She won. Like always. Any action here?"

"Sadie!" Mary Ann laughed. "Truth be told, I had some stiff competition this year, but I pulled off another blue ribbon."

"Congratulations." Liz turned to Sadie. "And no, there's been no 'action.'"

"Well, that's just disappointing."

"So far the history thief is lying low." Liz looked up at the large round clock mounted on the wall. "Time to get my cast together."

Mary Ann hugged her. "They'll do great."

"And if they don't," said Sadie, "we'll still clap anyway."

As usual, Sadie's no-nonsense tone set Liz at ease.

As her friends went outside, Liz clapped her hands. The sound caught the actors' attention and they gathered around.

"Okay, people. This is it. I appreciate all you've done to pull this together."

"And remember the details," Amber called out. "After we learn the outcome of today I'll be putting the final touches on my play. I've titled it *Theft and Secrets in Pleasant Creek.*"

Liz heard a few groans and felt the urge to join in. The title needed some work.

"Let's line up by the door. We start any minute."

As the group complied, Edna pulled Liz aside. "There are a couple of people missing."

"Really?"

"Claire and the man who thanks the three heroes for their service in saving the charter."

"Nope. I'm here," the man in question said as he jogged to the group. "Needed a pit stop."

"Has anyone heard from Claire?"

A few answered "no" or shook their heads in response.

"She probably got caught up in traffic," Amber said. "I had to park so far away I barely made it on time myself."

"If she gets here late, she can slide into place."

The front door opened and Jackson walked inside. Even in the heat of the day and with the pressure weighing on him, his blue polo shirt and creased khakis looked like he'd just walked out of the house. Only the shadows in his eyes gave away his mood.

"You're ready?" he asked Liz.

"As we'll ever be. You?"

He nodded. "The chief has his men stationed in different locations around the reenactment stage. The crowd is a pretty good size, but he's confident he can take care of any situation."

She blew out a breath.

"I'll announce the reenactment, then the actors can come out and begin. The historical marker presentation will come later."

Last-minute jitters gave Liz pause. "Are you sure we're doing the right thing?"

Jackson took hold of her hand and squeezed. "I guess we'll find out when it's over."

Waving to the cast, Jackson left.

"Okay everyone, the mayor will announce you in a few minutes. I'll be outside, just off to the left."

Amber gave Liz a thumbs-up. "It's normal to have excess nerves before a presentation," she reassured Liz.

"Thanks for your help. I couldn't have pulled this off without you." With one last look at the actors, Liz slipped out the front door.

The size of the crowd out front surprised her. She'd expected a large number, but the street was packed a few blocks in either direction. She could see far enough down Main Street to make out the tourists walking by the booths, speaking to merchants, and making purchases. But the crowd right before her looked expectantly toward the set. She crossed her fingers and waited.

Just then, Jackson's voice carried over the crowd. He made a few announcements, then introduced the reenactment of the signing of the original Pleasant Creek charter.

"That's our cue," she whispered.

One of the men opened the door and the actors filed out. They took their places. Kendell stepped up front and started the performance. His voice carried loud and clear, his exuberance for the part drawing in the people watching. He laid out the story as they'd rehearsed, with sweeping hand gestures and dramatic pauses.

Liz glanced at the crowd, pleased to see them transfixed by the story. Her gaze traveled to the far sides and back of the crowd, looking for what, she didn't know. She glimpsed Officer Hughes standing at attention, aware of the scene around him. Knowing the other officers were stationed out there helped alleviate some of her dread, but she kept waiting for someone to yell, or burst through the crowd, or heaven knew what.

She turned back to the actors, smiling when Edna stepped up to the "mayor" to take his arm. Liz had to admit she was having a good time, despite knowing that the history thief was out there somewhere, plotting his next move.

She'd just glanced back at the crowd when she noticed movement out of the corner of her eye. A tall, frowning man, unfamiliar to her, searched the crowd as he walked the perimeter. Liz tensed. She'd expected the history thief to be a local, but who knew for sure? She was just about to gesture to Jackson when the man's scowl broke into a smile and he wove his way through the people to stop beside a woman. He placed his arm around her shoulders and watched the entertainment.

Liz nearly doubled over with relief.

Before long, the charter was signed and the fake townsfolk applauded the heroes, prompting cheers from the audience. The actors took a quick bow from their places and moved off to the side. Jackson stepped to the front again.

"How was that for a little town history, folks? If you didn't know anything about Pleasant Creek, you know our humble beginnings now. You are also invited to venture deeper into our past by stopping by the courthouse lobby to view a display of Pleasant Creek history."

The crowd applauded again. Liz balled her hands into fists, her pulse racing. *What is the thief waiting for?*

"Thanks to the Pleasant Creek Playhouse actors for bringing history to life. And I'd also like to thank Liz Eckardt for directing the reenactment. Give it up for Liz."

She waved to the crowd, glad that Jackson hadn't asked her to speak. She could barely swallow. The suspense had made her queasy.

"We have another town ceremony we'd love you to stick around for." Jackson caught her eye, and she noticed his barely perceptible shrug, as if asking "Where is the thief?" She knew he was waiting too, his rigid stance the only giveaway of his uneasiness. "Chief Houghton?"

The chief climbed the steps and stood beside Jackson. Liz noticed his hand hovered near his firearm.

"As part of this year's festivities, a committee was assembled to take on the task of cleaning or upgrading the markers placed on historical buildings throughout town. It's important to keep history, and those who played a part in it, alive for future generations. Today, in honor of all the historical memorabilia being displayed in the courthouse lobby, we dedicate a new historical marker."

Jackson turned to accept the marker from his assistant. Still, no masked marauder burst through the crowd to fulfill his plan.

Disappointment and relief swamped Liz. Had this been a hoax? Had the thief made ongoing threats only to chicken out at the last minute? Had he ever planned to make an appearance?

Jackson turned, holding up a new, shiny square. "After much consideration, the courthouse lobby will now be called the Pleasant Creek History Center."

Applause broke out again. Residents of Pleasant Creek and tourists alike were delighted with the new name, if the hoots and hollers were any indication.

"You aren't taking away our family history," came a shout from the rear of the crowd. Before Jackson had a chance to respond, Liz heard the sharp report of explosions.

19

Shrieks mingled with the staccato explosions and bright flashes of light. People ran in all directions, trying to take cover. Parents grabbed their children, dragging them to find safety. In the chaos, no one knew if there were gunshots ringing out along with the gunpowder blasts. Smoke rose from the direction of the municipal park.

She crouched and ducked, her arms over her head as more blasts erupted. In the commotion, she noticed Jackson and the chief running through the crowd in the direction of the park.

Her heart pounded as she watched. Shouts carried over the din, and she remembered that someone had told her the fire department had stored the fireworks at the far end of the park for the show scheduled after the sun went down. Someone had set off the fireworks too soon.

The history thief.

From her peripheral vision, she saw Mary Ann leading Sadie to shelter. As the street cleared, people apparently began to realize the noise came from the fireworks, not gunfire. One by one, people rose from the positions to which they had dropped during the confusion. There was a lull in the cacophony, then another round of booming explosions started. Those who had risen dropped down again, including Liz. A siren blared in the distance as white smoke from the discharged fireworks wafted down Main Street. Minutes passed before the officers made their way down Main, asking those still lingering to make their way to the other end of the street. Still, there were those who stopped to look back and see what was going on.

From her vantage point on the steps, Liz saw Jackson threading his way through the crowd and back to the courthouse. She shivered, thinking of what he might be heading into so bravely. Even this far away she could see that he still exuded an air of authority. Liz had taken a few shaky steps intending to meet him when the doors of the courthouse flew open.

Thomas Sullivan appeared, a rifle cradled in his brawny arms.

Liz stopped in her tracks.

Thomas cocked the gun and fired into the air. Screams erupted from the crowd.

Jackson had come to an abrupt halt, his hands held out before him.

Thomas Sullivan yelled at Jackson. "No one is changing any building names today, or any day."

Jackson eased forward. "Thomas. We talked about this."

"No. You and your committee conspired to take away our heritage."

"You know that isn't true."

Thomas moved farther out on the stoop, the doors closing behind him. "You insisted on the change."

"To reflect the changing times. That's why we dedicated the lobby to the town."

"Lot of good that does us. Who cares about the lobby?"

"When it becomes a renowned historical center, lots of people will. You know it wasn't personal."

Thomas shook the gun. "Well I took it personal."

"Let's be reasonable."

"Reasonable? You want me to be reasonable?" He laughed. "First, you want to change the names on the buildings. What next, you wipe away any trace of the beginnings of Pleasant Creek? A town my ancestor fought for?"

Liz gulped as she watched Thomas's face go a deeper red. The man was hopelessly, desperately beyond all rational thought.

"That was never our intention," Jackson said, his voice calm. Liz marveled at her friend's ability to keep his composure.

Thomas shifted the rifle. "You mock my family's sacrifice."

As Liz turned her head to see Jackson's response, she saw police officers cautiously making their way toward the disturbance, firearms drawn and ready.

"What do you want, Thomas?"

"To get my history back."

"Fine. We can do as you ask."

His face darkened further. "Just like that? After all of your scheming, you just say okay and things go back to normal?"

"Yes," Jackson answered.

"I don't believe you. Why do you think I went to all this trouble?"

"What trouble?"

Thomas waved his free hand. "The reenactment. Setting the fireworks off early. I had to make a statement."

"You ordered the reenactment?"

The older man nodded.

"You stole the belongings from the folks around town?"

"No one listens until you take something away from them. It worked. I took your things and in return you made the reenactment happen."

"And now you got what you wanted, Thomas. A platform. A chance to air your grievances."

"Too little too late, Cross."

Oh no, Liz thought. He wasn't going to back down. His agitation seemed to grow with each passing second.

"Anyone who wants to change the courthouse name from Sullivan, they gotta come through me."

Before Jackson could respond, the police chief spoke up. "I'm afraid that's not possible, Thomas. Put down the gun. Don't make things worse than they already are."

"You expect me to put down my rifle just because you say so? Think again."

"There's no outcome that ends well if you don't surrender."

Thomas turned his gaze to Jackson. "You should have listened when I wanted to make the new markers."

"Why is that?"

Thomas looked around. "Claire? Claire!"

Claire rounded the side of the courthouse, her arms wrapped around a large object. She carried it to her husband.

He handed her the rifle, which she took with practiced ease, and he held up a huge, square plaque. From her spot, Liz could make out the name *Sullivan*.

"This will replace that bit of nothing you cleaned up to put back on the building."

"Fine, Thomas. We'll make sure it goes up."

"No you won't. *I* will. This here is the token everyone thought was lost after the ambush."

Thomas Sullivan had the original all along?

"My ancestor forged this when he opened the ironworks. He took it all the way to Indianapolis and brought it back with the charter. The first mayor never had it mounted on the courthouse. Now I'll make sure it's done right."

As the crowd watched Thomas wave his plaque around, Lilith walked up to the courthouse steps. "Thomas Sullivan, do you think your granddaddy would condone what you're doing here today?"

"Stay away, Lilith," Claire hissed.

"This is as much your fault," Thomas accused.

"How do you figure?"

"You didn't stick up for our history. Didn't join the committees that wanted to make changes and try to stop them. You turned a blind eye."

"Ever heard the expression 'you can't fight city hall'?"

"I went about it the right way but no one listened."

"And by 'the right way,' you mean scaring people and stealing their belongings?"

Claire barked out a laugh. "You're one to talk."

Lilith stumbled. Sadie rushed over to clasp her hand in Lilith's. Liz's heart clenched at the show of solidarity.

"I made it look like you took the wagon wheel," Thomas confessed. "Sent those pictures so everyone would think you were guilty."

Gasps burst around her. When she looked at Lilith, Liz saw Sadie tugging her friend away from the attention. Worried, Liz rose, ready to move in their direction.

Lilith's mouth dropped open as the truth hit home. "You set fire to my barn?"

"Even if the original wheel was destroyed, at least I made the new one to take its place outside the courthouse. This town remains indebted to my family."

"But history wasn't made by your family alone," said Lilith.

"There are no more Oateses. None of the Granger clan except for you lives in town. The Sullivans can make their claim now."

"Claim to what?"

Thomas lowered the plaque to rest against the building and took the rifle back. He aimed it at the crowd. "Whatever we want."

By now, the officers had crept closer to the scene playing out before the entire town. No one had expected Heritage Day to turn into such a spectacle.

"It's time for some changes, and the government isn't going to be the one making them."

"Neither are you," Chief Houghton said.

"We'll see about that." Thomas whispered something in his wife's ear. She nodded, turned, and made her way down the steps. As she drew closer, Liz realized she was headed in her direction. She felt her knees go weak with terror.

Claire grabbed her arm and pulled Liz jerkily up the steps while Thomas kept the gun trained on her. Liz held up her hands, not wanting to do anything more to offend the man with his finger on the trigger.

Jackson and the police chief started moving forward but stopped when Thomas fired a warning shot into the air.

"Seems to me a hostage is always a useful thing," Thomas said to Liz when Claire pushed her his way.

"Or a dangerous one," Liz said. She sounded more confident than she felt.

Thomas laughed. "Always thought you had a bit of grit about you. Did a good job on the reenactment."

"Really? This doesn't seem like an appropriate way to thank me." She eyed the rifle in his hand.

"Just want you to know I appreciate it. You did my family proud."

Liz pressed her lips together instead of blurting what she thought his ancestors might say if they could see him now. Sarcasm was not going to defuse the situation. She glanced over at her friends, meeting Jackson's steady gaze. He nodded slightly, as if to reassure her. It was a promise she feared he couldn't keep in his current unarmed condition.

"So what now, Thomas?" Jackson asked.

"Now we go over my list of demands."

Liz's eyes went wide. *More demands?*

"First, all the buildings in town will bear the Sullivan name."

Hadn't he just said no name changes to any of the buildings in town? *The man is losing it.*

Jackson's eyes tightened in the corners, but he nodded in agreement.

"Secondly, we don't go to jail."

The chief opened his mouth to speak, but Liz blurted, "I'm an attorney."

Thomas gazed down at her. "You'll help us out here?"

She lifted her shoulders. "I could try."

"See that, chief? Got me a lawyer."

She had never practiced criminal law, nor was she even licensed in Indiana, but she decided not to mention those pesky details.

"Third, you make sure that reenactment gets done every Heritage Day."

Jackson took a step forward. "I agree. Now let Liz go."

"You're a smart man. You know that's not how this works."

"Oh, for heaven's sake," Lilith said. "Stop the grandstanding and just give up."

"My granddaddy never gave up. Neither will I."

"If he'd crafted that wagon correctly to begin with, we wouldn't be talking about this."

"What did you say?"

"You heard me." Lilith placed her hands on her hips. "My granddaddy said yours didn't connect the wheel tight enough to the axle when they left town. It was only a matter of time before the thing fell off."

Thomas's face turned an unhealthy red again. "That's an outright lie."

"Which you have no way to prove. It's your word against mine."

"I'm the one holding the gun, so my word is the only one that counts."

"Until this is all over. Then I'll make sure everyone knows what a poor craftsman your granddaddy was."

Thomas took a step toward Lilith but Claire grabbed his arm. "Remember the bigger prize here, honey."

"You can't silence me, Thomas Sullivan," Lilith said.

Thomas clamped his mouth shut but continued to glare at Lilith.

"Here's what we're going to do," Claire said. "The three of us are going inside. There, we will wait until the police clear the street. We will then go home and we'll act like this was just another fine day in Pleasant Creek."

Great, Liz thought. *They've both lost their minds.*

Voices rose again as the police yelled for the Sullivans to freeze, but Claire was already tugging Liz backward. She struggled, but Claire whispered, "I have a gun in my purse, and I know how to use it."

Liz froze momentarily, then felt herself pushed forward. She didn't know anything about guns, but this woman looked like she knew her way around firearms. Liz wasn't about to put her to the test.

Thomas held up the rifle in front of him, inching backward. Liz knew that disappearing indoors was probably the worst thing that could happen, but what could she do? Claire had threatened her, and Thomas didn't seem like he'd listen to reason, even from his would-be lawyer. She thought about accidentally tripping or faking a heart attack, when the door to the courthouse was pushed open from inside.

It took Liz a moment to realize what had just happened. Her gaze met Claire's, and just as Liz made a move to escape, the door opened wider, pushing Liz right into her captor.

Claire's eyes went wide and she teetered, straight into the back of her husband. With a heavy push, Liz sent Claire careening. Thomas made a sound of surprise and lowered the gun when he, too, lost his balance.

The last thing Liz heard before bedlam reigned was Bert's voice as he popped his head out the door and asked, "Am I interrupting here?"

20

Chaos erupted yet again.

Jackson rushed Thomas, catching him off guard. He wrested the gun from the hands of the big man. The chief shouted commands while quickly swooping in to take control of the situation. Claire argued with Officer Gerst, who tried to get her into cuffs while she struggled.

"She has a gun," Liz warned.

The officer immediately snapped on the cuffs and pushed Claire up against the building to search her. He found the gun and handed it to Officer Dixon, who had run over to assist him. Between the chief and the officers, they turned the situation from deadly to under control in no time.

As the crowd settled down, Liz watched the officers march the cuffed prisoners away. Relief flooded her. There would be plenty of questions, but they would have to wait. All that mattered right now was that every man, woman, and child within the courthouse perimeter was safe.

"Come this way." Naomi waved to the remaining crowd. "Free cupcakes."

The merchants cajoled the crowd back into the area of the booths, offering giveaways. Pleasant Creek then showed its true colors: warm, friendly people willing to offer comfort to the tourists.

Liz worked her way through the crowd to find Sadie, Mary Ann, and Lilith. The three wore shell-shocked expressions, but were no worse for the wear. Liz hugged them.

"You're okay?" she asked.

"Other than being scared out of our wits, we survived," Mary Ann said, her voice shaky.

"Always did think Thomas Sullivan had a screw loose," Sadie said.

"At least the police were able to stop them." Liz turned to Lilith. "And you, standing up to him. What were you thinking?"

"To be honest, I'm not sure. My feet moved and my mouth followed."

The women laughed, the jitters starting to melt away.

"Glad someone sees the humor in the situation."

Liz spun around to see Jackson, a grimace on his face. The pressure in her chest eased. "And you were pretty quick on your feet too. I almost thought you might be able to reason with Thomas."

He shrugged, relief evident in his eyes. "I had to try."

Sadie walked over and patted Jackson's cheek. "Wouldn't expect anything less, Jackson."

The three women left, leaving Liz alone with the mayor.

"Please don't ever do that again," Liz told him, looking deep into his hazel eyes.

"What? Try to diffuse a tense situation?"

"Put yourself in the line of fire."

"I didn't think he'd shoot me."

Liz raised a brow.

"Okay, I hoped he wouldn't."

"You took ten years off my life."

"Me? I nearly came unglued when Thomas took you hostage."

They both fell silent.

"How about we both promise not to worry each other like that again?" Liz suggested.

"Not sure either of us can make that promise."

Liz shook her head, a begrudging grin curving her lips.

"Besides, why do you care so much?" he asked.

How could she answer when she wasn't quite sure herself? Jackson was handsome, loyal, and quick to make her smile. But she told herself time and time again that he was just a good friend, nothing more. This was not the time or place to analyze her feelings for the man standing before her, so she brushed away his question with a flick of her hand.

"No one runs Pleasant Creek better than you, Mayor Cross. What would we do without you?"

"The town would survive."

"I beg to differ."

He stepped closer, a smile playing at his lips. "Then maybe we should—"

"What happens now?" She cut in, not ready for any personal revelations. "It looks like the fire department has cordoned off the park."

Jackson shot her a look that said, *We aren't finished with this conversation*, then turned in the direction of the commotion a few blocks away. "The park's a mess. Guess we'll have to cancel the picnic. And there won't be any fireworks since it looks like Sullivan set off the lot." He looked at her again. "Any suggestions?"

She thought about it for a moment, then inspiration struck. "How about we move the picnic to the grounds of the inn? After today's excitement, I'll bet most tourists will head home. There should be plenty of space for the townspeople to spread out over my property."

"I like the idea. Let me see what the status is with the food vendors to find out if your idea works."

"Of course it'll work."

He chuckled. "Pretty *and* modest."

She felt her cheeks flush.

"I should probably get over there and find out what's going on." He moved a step away, but stopped and turned back to look at her. "I appreciate you taking care of the reenactment for me, Liz. It took a load off my mind because I knew you could handle it."

"Thanks for believing in me."

"You proved yourself to be a true Pleasant Creek citizen today."

"I'll take that compliment anytime."

As he walked away, Liz blew out a deep breath. The excitement might be over, but she still had work to do.

———————

After much finagling, the town picnic was moved to the grounds of the Olde Mansion Inn. Multicolored blankets dotted the soft green grass. Children ran about, playing supervised games while women readied food for the hungry crowd. The tantalizing aroma of burgers on the grill made Liz's mouth water. The atmosphere had gone from one of alarm to one of joyous celebration. The evening sky turned lovely shades of orange and lavender as the sun made its nightly descent.

Liz went about greeting her friends, thankful they were safe and accounted for. Opal and her husband sat with the members of the train club, and Opal waved as Liz walked by. Caitlyn had been called in to the hospital. The Hastingses, both couples, sat with the group of actors, laughing while Edna held court.

Liz had just turned back toward the inn when she noticed Miriam and Philip hovering by the side of the house. She headed over.

"Welcome. Have you come to join the celebration?"

"I am afraid not. We only wanted to contribute to the picnic." Miriam turned as Philip pulled a small wagon toward them. "We had homemade pickles left over from the sales today. After the way the town pitched in and took care of each other, we wanted to do our part."

"How thoughtful."

Philip nodded his head toward the long tables and pulled the wagon in that direction.

"It is you we must thank," Miriam rushed to say. "I know you were concerned about the reenactment, but from what I heard, your team did a good job."

"They did. Until Thomas decided to make his statement."

"At least all ended well."

Liz looked over at Philip talking to Jackson. "How did you get him to stop here?"

A smile graced Miriam's face. "It was simple. Philip has a big heart, even though he does not always show it."

"You know what? I believe you."

"Our communities may be very different, but we all love Pleasant Creek."

The Borkholders took their leave after Philip unloaded the jars. Working her way toward her friends, she found Mary Ann, Sadie, Naomi, and Lilith seated in lawn chairs, an empty chair awaiting Liz. She plopped down with a contented sigh.

Naomi smiled at her. "It was nice of you to offer your property for the picnic."

"With what the town went through today, we deserved a party. A change of location was not going to stand in the way."

"It didn't take the parks department long to get those long tables here, and then for folks to fill every surface with food." Sadie looked down at her empty plate. "I think I indulged more than I should have."

"That's what people do on holidays," Mary Ann said.

"Well I'm happy to get a piece of your blueberry pie," Lilith said as she polished off the last bite. "Made today's nonsense worthwhile."

"Speaking of which," Sadie said. "I will never get over you deciding to stand up to Thomas Sullivan."

"At first I was just plain angry. He had some nerve, hiding the wagon wheel to make me look guilty, then burning down my barn. Holding people at gunpoint? Unacceptable. I didn't think, I just spoke."

"You sure knew how to get his goat."

Lilith shrugged. "I've known the Sullivans a long time. Knew which buttons to push."

"For which we are extremely grateful," Naomi said. "I was pretty far from the action, but trust me, I felt the panic from the crowd. We didn't know if we should run to help or stay put."

"So how did you decide what to do?" Liz asked.

"The first gunshot blast kept us at our booths," Naomi answered.

"There wasn't a thing you could have done," Sadie went on to say. "Thomas was on a rampage, but Lilith," she patted her friend's arm, "she stepped in and saved the day."

"Certainly not. The hero is Bert."

Liz chuckled. "The expression on his face was priceless. The poor man probably won't leave the courthouse for weeks now."

"I was happy to do my part," Lilith said. "My granddaddy always insisted Sullivan didn't build the wagon right. I just played up on the old grudge between our families."

"It was perfect. You were the star of the show."

A humble expression came over Lilith's face. "You know, I don't think I've nailed a role like that in years. It must be my best performance yet."

The women laughed. If that was Lilith's final act, she'd outdone herself.

As the sun set, a local band set up a portable stage and started playing country tunes. In lieu of fireworks, Jackson had somehow gotten hold of sparklers, which were passed out to the children. In the distance, residents from different locations in town shot off cascading rockets into the inky sky. The beautiful colors were mirrored in Jaynes Lake, which was located behind the inn. Exclamations of awe and the sound of lively music filled the night. Liz couldn't think of a better way to end the day.

Just before ten o'clock, when it looked like the local families would be heading home, Amber and Kendell took over the band microphones.

"What's going on?" Liz asked.

Mary Ann shrugged. "Beats me."

Amber blew on the microphone to make sure it was working. "First, I want to thank the town of Pleasant Creek for sticking together. This is my first Fourth of July celebration here and I have to say, there's no way you'll be able to match this year's festivities."

The crowd laughed and hooted.

"Today's events have given me material for my next play, so keep that in mind when the Pleasant Creek Playhouse brings you an adaptation of the events." Her bangles clattered noisily as she waved her hand. "But enough from me. Tonight, we have a special announcement to make."

Amber took a step back and handed the mic over to Kendell. "There are times when a town comes together under trying circumstances. Pleasant Creek has weathered an experience we won't soon forget. In those times of uncertainty, we look to a person who shines bright in the darkness of adversity. Tonight, we would like to honor that person." He searched the crowd until his gaze landed on his target. "Lilith Granger, please join us."

"Me?" Lilith gasped.

"Your public awaits," Sadie urged, a twinkle in her eye.

Lilith rose and slowly made her way to the stage. Kendell took her arm to help her up. Confusion crossed her face as she stood next to the pair.

"Lilith, you took on Thomas Sullivan, even at the expense of your own safety. We can't thank you enough for distracting him until Bert opened the courthouse door."

Clapping filled the night. Several chanted, "Bert, Bert," until the older man stood and took a quick bow.

"In honor of your sacrifice of your own safety, we've formed a committee of volunteers who are going to come out and paint your house, do repairs, and cut your grass."

"No, no," Lilith gushed, but her shocked expression soon turned to one of pleasure.

"Yes," Amber countered. "You've helped many of us in the past. Sometimes we forget that our neighbors need a helping hand from time to time. You aren't invisible, Lilith. It's our time to return the favor."

Everyone stood and applauded. Lilith looked shocked, but her eyes swam with grateful tears. There might not have been a fireworks show lighting the starry night this year, but Liz was sure most folks would go home with a sense of contentment in their hearts. Lilith's family home would be restored. She wouldn't have to worry about managing the upkeep on her own. This was the true legacy of Pleasant Creek.

"So, did you have anything to do with this volunteer committee?" Liz asked as she leaned close to Sadie's ear.

"Might have made a few calls. Put a few ideas in people's heads."

Liz circled her arm around Sadie's shoulders. "You are a good woman, Sadie Schwarzentruber."

Sadie shrugged, but her voice was raspy when she said, "Don't you forget it."

After the announcement, the crowd began to pack up for home. Other than the tables, which would be picked up tomorrow, it was as if there had been no celebration here at all. Her friends, having said good night, headed off. Liz carried a trash bag to the can on the side of the inn, noticing Jackson and Chief Houghton standing at the end of the parking lot, deep in conversation.

Rubbing her arms against a trickle of unease, Liz made her way in their direction. Jackson saw her first and stopped speaking.

"Oh no. You aren't going to leave me out of the loop, are you?"

The chief frowned.

"If you didn't want to arouse my curiosity, you should have had this conversation at the station."

The corner of Jackson's mouth quirked. "She has a point."

"What's going on?" Liz pressed.

"You'll find out soon enough," the chief said, heaving a sigh of resignation. "We've questioned the Sullivans and searched their house. There is no sign of the stolen items."

21

The following weekend, the town showed up full force to take care of Lilith's house. Loaded with paint buckets, scrapers, saws, fresh wood, and lawn mowers, the townspeople descended on the property, and the house and lawn soon buzzed with activity. Liz hurried about the kitchen, making sure there was plenty of cold water for the volunteers. Mary Ann made sandwiches. They'd been busy since eight, making sure there was enough food and drink to go around.

"Lilith is still in shock," Mary Ann said as she slathered mustard on a slice of bread. "But staying at Sadie's has been wonderful for both of them."

"I'm happy they've mended fences. No one should have to weather life's storms alone."

"And no one will have to as long as I'm around," Sadie declared as she walked into the kitchen wearing a ball cap and a whistle hanging around her neck. "As for the workers outside, they're right on schedule."

Mary Ann bagged another sandwich. "We knew you were the perfect person to marshal the troops."

"One of my many talents."

Liz was just about to take ice from the freezer when Lilith walked into the kitchen holding up some booklets. "Look what I found."

"Playbills?" Sadie guessed.

"Yes." She chuckled. "Look at this awful picture." She held open a page for the women to see. Under heavy makeup and a wig, Lilith posed in a flowing gown.

"Lady Macbeth?" Mary Ann guessed.

"I could never resist Shakespeare."

"When was this?" Liz asked.

"Shortly after the playhouse opened. My first big role."

"It was also when I started working on the costumes," Sadie said. "I remember we had lots of fun."

Lilith's grin faded. "Until I got too bigheaded and ruined our friendship."

Sadie shrugged. "The important thing is that we're friends now." She hugged Lilith. "I'm happy we're talking again."

"So am I," came Lilith's teary reply.

"Where did you find the pamphlets?" Mary Ann asked.

"In the study. I have tons of stuff that I really need to weed out. Boxes. Boxes inside boxes. A hope chest buried under boxes. It's going to be an ordeal."

"So what better time than the present?" Sadie suggested in a tone that was a tad bossy, even though her smile revealed she had Lilith's best interests at heart.

"Are you sure?"

"Folks are busy outside; we can get busy in here." Sadie turned. "You in, girls?"

Liz and Mary Ann exchanged glances.

"Why not?" Liz answered.

As the others moved to the study, Liz scooped ice into a cooler and carried it to the backyard. She'd just set it down when the chief strolled her way. He sported a T-shirt and worn jeans.

"Here to lend a hand?"

He nodded. "I'm hoping some physical work will help me think events through. We still haven't found the stolen items."

Liz shook her head. "What is the Sullivans' excuse for not giving you the information?"

"We didn't give them what they wanted."

"I still can't believe they went to all that trouble to steal from the town, and got away with it for as long as they did. No one noticed."

"They were pretty sneaky. Claire did most of the work. She could move freely in and out of stores without looking suspicious or out of place. Thomas was the mastermind, though, upset about his forefathers not being honored. He had a chip on his shoulder long before this plot to take matters into their own hands. I think the building name change pushed him over the edge."

"There's no way to get him to reveal his hiding place?"

"Nothing so far. The only thing he said is that he stored everything in a place we'd least expect it."

"Which could be anywhere. Let's hope they get a conscience and reveal the hiding place."

"I've known Thomas a long time. He's as stubborn as they come. Only thing he'd admit to was the letter he sent to the courthouse threatening us. Claire came up with the idea to send Sadie the letter, drawing her into the intrigue and pointing the finger of blame at Lilith. And she set off the fireworks before joining her husband on the courthouse steps. Those two outdid themselves." The chief hitched up his pants. "Now I'm off to get some work done."

"Me too. See you later."

Liz went back inside, joining the ladies in the study. They'd already removed the boxes from on top of the hope chest.

"I can't remember what's inside," Lilith said. "It's been forever since I came in here."

"It'll be a walk down memory lane." Sadie placed the last box on the floor. "Go ahead. Open it up."

Lilith skirted the boxes and stood before the lovely wooden hope chest. She ran a finger over the rich mahogany before slipping her fingers under the lip to lift the top. She peered inside, and a frown creased her forehead.

Sadie moved closer. "Fond memories?"

"More like confusion." Lilith looked up. "I don't recognize a thing."

Liz came up to the chest and knelt beside it. "Maybe these are your mother's things?"

"Not at all." Lilith began to rummage through the chest.

"Wait," Mary Ann called out. "There's the thimble set that went missing from the shop."

"And Naomi's sign." Liz removed it.

Before long they'd cleared space on the floor to lay out the contents of the chest.

"The stolen belongings," Mary Ann declared.

"Must be." Sadie looked over the assortment of possessions. "But how did they get here?"

"Don't look at me," Lilith said. "I haven't been in here in ages."

"But the chief searched your house. He wouldn't have missed this."

"After the fire I stayed at your house, Sadie. Anyone could have broken into my house to hide the items. Thomas put the wheel in my barn to make me look guilty. Why not come back and plant these antiques too?"

The women stared at the haul for a long moment. Liz broke the silence. "This is everything?"

"Seems to be. Why?" Mary Ann asked.

"I don't see my inkwell."

The women searched, but came up empty.

"The officers at the station have a complete list. They'll have to compare and see if all the stolen goods are here."

Liz let out a breath. "Guess I should let the chief know we solved the last piece of the puzzle."

————————— //////////////////////// —————————

After a thorough search, only a few items were still missing, one of them Liz's inkwell. She tried not to let it bother her, but she had to admit she was disappointed. The gift had meant a lot to her and, now, thanks to the history thief and his attempt to rewrite history, it was gone. Maybe forever.

On a Tuesday night a few weeks later, the Material Girls gathered in Sew Welcome to finish up the pencil case project. After forming an assembly line to complete the job, the women took a break. Beans waddled around the room, lapping up the attention of the chatting women.

"I heard the Sullivans finally confessed to their deeds," Sadie said, opening a cardboard box to hold their handiwork.

"How could they keep quiet any longer when the truth came out?" Opal smoothed the fabric on one of the bags. "I don't care what their excuse was, they should have acted like adults and expressed their grievances in a mature manner."

"Just goes to show, age has nothing to do with one's ability to act like a five-year-old who's lost his marbles on the playground," Sadie added.

"Marbles?" Caitlyn laughed. "How about video games?"

"You get the idea."

"I do and I agree. This whole thing could have been avoided if they'd just spoken to someone about their concerns instead of harboring bitterness."

"It's over now. Everyone got their belongings ba—" Mary Ann stopped and cringed. "Sorry, Liz."

"At this point I'm not expecting to get the inkwell back. Who knows, maybe in their haste to frame Lilith, the Sullivans dropped it along the way."

Sadie glowered. "Still doesn't make it right."

"I've been looking online to find another, but even if I find a replacement, it won't be part of Pleasant Creek history," Liz said.

"How about I look for a new one?" Naomi offered. "We can wrap it up and present it to you just like before."

Liz chuckled. "It wouldn't be the same, but thanks for the offer."

Caitlyn glanced at her watch. "Let's get moving here. I still have to drop off the box tonight."

In a flurry of motion, the group packed and cleaned up. Before they had a chance to close up shop, the doorbell rang at the front door of the inn. Beans barked from his position by Liz's feet.

"Expecting guests this late?" Naomi asked.

"No. I'll be right back."

Liz exited the shop and walked to the foyer. She opened the front door to find Jackson on the porch.

"Hey. What're you doing here?"

"I have some good news." He grinned. "For a change."

Liz stepped out into the humid night to join him. The buzz of insects filled the otherwise quiet night. A streetlight glowed in the distance. Down the street, a car horn honked.

"Okay. Lay it on me."

Jackson stood with his hands behind his back. "The chief told me he'd gotten every ounce of information the Sullivans were going to give. They didn't recall your inkwell, so out of curiosity I went out to Lilith's property this afternoon and walked the perimeter of the house."

"I thought the officers did a thorough search after we opened the hope chest."

"They did, but between the search and all the folks working on the house, I thought maybe your inkwell might have been overlooked."

"If it was even there."

"It was." He brought his hands from behind his back and held the cobalt blue inkwell in his outstretched palms.

Liz gasped. "Jackson. How . . . Where?"

"Lilith's yard. Hidden among the shrubs, if you could call those sorry things shrubs. I focused on looking in and around them and found the inkwell wedged between a pretty gnarly root and the foundation of the house, underneath a window. That may have been where Thomas entered the house to hide the stolen items." He moved his hands closer. "Take it."

She did, cradling it in her hands. "I don't know what to say, besides thank you."

"I knew this memento meant a lot to you."

"This is beyond the call of duty."

"What can I say? I like seeing you smile."

The air grew heavy between them.

"So, that's it," Jackson said. "Just wanted to return your inkwell."

"I owe you."

"After taking on the reenactment, I'd say we're even."

"Sounds good to me."

Jackson backed away then turned and headed down the sidewalk. Liz felt a flutter in her stomach as she watched him leave.

"Liz," Mary Ann called from inside.

Liz retraced her steps.

"We're finished," Sadie said as the women gathered in the foyer.

"The store is closed for the night, so we're off," Mary Ann chimed in.

"Who stopped by so late?" Naomi asked.

"Jackson." Liz held up the inkwell. "He found it, so there's no need to search for a replacement."

"Awesome," Caitlyn said, hefting the box of pencil cases in her arms.

"Now we can put the entire business behind us," Sadie stated.

Liz held up the inkwell. In the overhead light, the blue glass sparkled. "Now that we have the past returned, we can look forward to a hopeful future."

Beans barked in agreement.

Learn more about Annie's fiction books at

AnniesFiction.com

- Access your e-books
- Discover exciting new series
- Read sample chapters
- Watch video book trailers
- Share your feedback

We've designed the Annie's Fiction website especially for you!

Plus, manage your account online!

- Check your account status
- Make payments online
- Update your address

Visit us at AnniesFiction.com